Knights Are No More

Jeanette Thomas

authorHOUSE®

AuthorHouse™
1663 Liberty Drive
Bloomington, IN 47403
www.authorhouse.com
Phone: 1 (800) 839-8640

Published by AuthorHouse 02/07/2017

ISBN: 978-1-5246-7039-9 (sc)
ISBN: 978-1-5246-7038-2 (e)

Print information available on the last page.

This book is printed on acid-free paper.

Chapter One

Her own scream woke her to the deafening silence in the room. What had she done? Dejection was settling in all at once. Why had it been so final. The papers were signed and the plans made. She could not turn back from the pull that lured her into the unknown. It would never be the same again not since her mom and dad were gone . . . never back like it had been. Never in the safety of her parents home. They were Gone . . . gone, and the house had been sold.

She had to be out of her childhood home by the end of the month. The sale was final. But today she would be gone, and starting her new life. Calls had been made and arrangements were finalized. My future waits. Why had she started to feel this pending doom around her with every move? Had she been wrong all her life? Was this just a childish dream? Had her dreams not been real? Had her love for castles taken it toll and pulled her away from sanity and the real world? She looked at the clock on the bedside stand, two am.

She could not start her day this early. The activities of the day would be tiring enough. And the house was empty except for her bed and trunk. The bed stayed but the trunk held what would be the start of her new life. Her dreams had come true but still the feeling of doom was there. She couldn't shake it.

She had to meet with the board. Her lawyer and adviser was going to the meeting with her. Donel had tried to persuade her to keep her stock and just let her lawyer manage it for her. But she wanted nothing to do with the legacy her father had left her. He was gone and would not be hurt by her decision. No, she would sell.

Maybe there would be enough capital form the sale to help in the restoration of the castle and begin her school. A writing school. A school of fine arts.

The trunk standing in the corner with its lid open brought fear again. When the top was closed and locked, it would be the end of life as she had known for these twenty-eight years. Everything sh owned was in that trunk, except for her books and computer. They had been shipped ahead and were waiting at her destination, all else had been sold. Her new life would began with just a few of her favorite treasures from her life with her parents. Mother's words still rang in the stillness of the room.

"you know knights are no more, Calista. Your love for castles will take you in the direction you don't want to go."

Why had she not listened to those words of warning? Mother's words were always right, were they not? The words had come the day she came home with the book tucked under arms from the library, 'Ancient Castles'. Her mother had picked it up, shook her head in dismay and gave her the warning.

Calista felt like a small child again wanting the protection of parents, and security of a loving home. So much of her mother was still here within these walls, even though the house stood empty. She could almost smell the sweet cinnamon rolls as they baked. The bright green gingham curtains that framed the windows still hung there. All was the same except the soft sound of her mother's voice singing a ballad or lullaby.

Calista's father had wanted her to take over his place on the board. Yet he had never let her sit in the board room with him. She had inherited the stock and held fifty nine percent of the company, which was of no interest to her. She had studied to be a teacher of writing, dreamed also of having her own school. If she was to sit on a board, it would be her own board. Director of her own school. To teach writing, and how it would take all senses to make a good manuscript. Create her own characters, make them do and act as she herself called the shots. Manipulate the romances, chose who was to love whom. And where else could such romances be formed except in a castle setting? In the age of romance, chivalry and high society.

Her love for castles had taken her in this direction. She had taken the insurance money from her parents accident and used most of it to purchase a castle, sight unseen, just pictures. She felt that she got such a bargain because no one wanted the castle which was a pile of rubble.

There were the pictures of the before the wars and after, but it could be restored in time. Most of the damage had been done during the wars and it had been uninhabited for more than fifty years. What had the sales add said, "all modern utilities could be arranged." This was the age of science and electronics. What would one do without a computer, research and email? Though she knew most of her writings would be about her dreams.

This was not something she wanted to do on a whim. She had dreamed of it, planned it since she couldn't remember when. It had been the biggest part of her waking dreams. To own her own castle. Write her own books. Why was fear overtaking her now? Her new life . . . new life . Sleep slipped in again and she was in her dream world.

She stood on a high hill and looked down. . . down to the great castle, her castle, new home. It was starting to get dark with the storm that hung in the distance. A storm in the shape of a dragon. And so cold, a cold that seeped into her very soul. She could smell the sulfur in the air from the lightening. Was the dragon protecting the castle or was it the enemy and the pending doom that engulfed her?

The rose bush she had planted in the corner of the herb garden was in bloom. The white roses in the twilight looked like a thousand waiting eyes protruding from the giant black monster. Waiting for her return.

"Calista . . . Calista . . . knights are no more . . . knights are no more. No knight is going to rescue you when trouble comes."

A light was on in her castle room. She hadn't left one on. Who could be there? She, living alone . . . no one should be in the whole castle, let alone in her room. Great fear was seeping into her very soul. She had never been afraid before. Yes, she had read where ghosts, goblins, and witches haunted castles, why would any of them have need of a light? They wouldn't . . . someone was in her castle. A dark shadow fell across the lawn form the light of the window. Danger loomed in the sky and danger awaited her in the cold stone edifice. She shivered at the cold that she felt.

She could see the figure as it marched about her room, almost in a cadence. Waiting . . . waiting for her return. Or the return of those living in the past before the wars . . .ghosts. Were they ghosts from the wars?

This was her dream, her fairy tale. If she wanted to conquer the dragon, the bush monster or the ghost of a shadow in her room all she had to do was wake up. This was her dream and had no control over her. A hand touched her shoulder and she tensed to the cold touch. The touch was unreal. Her very strength was challenged. When she turned with fight in her fisted hands there was no one there . . . no one!

Calista woke tense and with her fists drawn to fight. How did you fight with ghosts? Where had the ghosts come from? Her life had been very secure. Why did her mind harbor ghosts? She was wet with sweat but cold. It was June she shouldn't be cold. Remembering her dream she realized why she was ready to fight. And how cold the storm had been. A slight fear slipped into her mind, had it really been a dream or had she been carried away out of reality with a warning? A warning that danger was waiting for her in her new castle home. The castle wasn't new, it was heaped in ruins but it was her new home. Yes, castles were not new to her, she had read everything she could find on them. Each thought brought a rebuttal to her confused mind.

She had read and reread all the papers that the realtor had sent about her castle... L . Belthasar Castle. The king had given it to the high knight of his army. Had made him lord and gave him the castle. A castle set on five hundred acres of rich ferile soil. The land had been tilled by the servants for the Balthasar family and had belonged to them until the wars. It had fallen to the empire when seemingly all the Balthasar were killed or escaped for their lives, it was put up for sale and on one seemed to want it. Now it was hers.

In her research she had found the Balthasar heirs. There were two of them still in existence, that she had found. Dugan Balthasar the oldest and an heir, and his sister, Ceara Balthasar. Why had they not claimed their inheritance? Was this also a warning for her? What had she done? Why did none of the local residents want this home? Why did Dugan and Ceara not want it? Was she the only foolish one? All because of her childhood dreams, of being an owner of a castle.

Calista took her shower and dressed for the board meeting. Folded her few things and put them in the trunk. Folded her bed clothes and placed them on top, to protect her things. She tried to close the lid with care but it became heavy and dropped from her hands with a bang. She jumped back as if something had taken the lid from her. Closed and locked it stood as a symbol of the end, waiting to be taken away. She picked up the stock papers and left for the last time. She didn't look back. The movers were to pick up the trunk and take it to the train.

She stepped form the taxi in front of the biggest real estate anency in the area. She looked up at the tall building. How she had wanted to go into that building with her father when she was a small child. When she wasn't dreaming of knights and castles she dreamed of being a high executive for the company, after all she held the controlling stocks in her hand. Now she was going into the board room for her father. A hand grasped her elbow gently.

"Calista . . . I knew one day you would sit on the board with me."

"Kemp Maston! What a suprise. I had forgotten you were with the company."

She took the opportunity of him holding her elbow to put her hand across her stomach which began to twist in knots form nerves. She wasn't really interested in Kemp Maston. He had hit on her when they were in high school. And she was no more interested then, than she was now.

He had been the one always to push for the best grades, always wanting more . . . better . . . to be the best. Calista had been lost in her own fantasy world, living a magical dream, not ready ready for a serious relationship. Even if she had been it wouldn't be Kemp Maston she would have dreamed of. Not the kind of relationship Kemp had wanted.

"As for me sitting on the board with you I am only here for this meeting. I am moving. My lawyer will be controlling my stock for me and sitting on the board in my place."

Calista patted the purse hanging on her hip. She had Kemp's future right here in this little leather bag. A smile went across her face unseen. She was in control of his future. Her stock would give him the controlling interest in the company. She couldn't help but feel he was more interested in her stock than he was her. Yes, when her stock went up for bid, Kemp would bid and probably buy. Pushing for more would give him more. She took the hand of the man that had just joined them.

"Good morning, Calista. I think you should reconsider this. Can I not persuade you?" He pulled her aside and tried. Kemp didn't go ahead he waited, inching closer and closer as they whispered.

"Afraid not, Donel. My mind is made up. I will leave on the two o'clock train."

Kemp's ears opened wide and his eyes showed interest. He has no idea what we are talking about, thought Calista, but he is very interested. He would be as surprised as the rest of the board when she gave her little speech that she had rehearsed in her mind over and over.

She turned to Donel, "I will send you my email address and mailing address as soon as I get settled in. I'm sure it won't be long."

. "May I have your email address?" Kemp took a piece of paper from his pocket and wrote down a message and handed it to her. Four pens she almost smiled to herself. Pens in the vest pocket showed authority . . . importance . . . that was always her thought. Was Kemp so important to the company to have four? She had always teased her father by adding more pens to his pocket as he left or work.

"This is my email address. Write as soon as you can."

"I'll be pretty busy for awhile." She made excuses.

Kemp was pushing her by the elbow hurrying her on. She pulled away and took hold of the hand rail for support. He wasn't going to push her, she thought. She could do this by herself. Stepping in front of her lawyer she led the way and let the lawyer come between her and Kemp. How she wished her father had brought her here so she would be familiar with the board room and the proceedings of the board.

As she stepped into the room the members of the board stood with their hands on the chair backs. The smell of freshly polished leather perfumed the room. They waited until everyone had chosen a place to sit. The shuffle of feet and pulling of the chairs in place did notheing to help Calista's nerves. Kemp had placed her between her lawyer and himself.

The chairman brought the meeting to order and read the minutes of the last meeting. Old business was discussed and Calista watched each face. Yes, this was a *bored* meeting, she smiled so deep within that it almost reached her face. Just wait until the floor is open for new business.

She patted her purse again. This will bring life to the members. They were expecting her to take her father's place. She knew they thought she was young and inexperienced and that they could control her. Surprise!

The chairman picked up the gavel and hit the block of wood, ending the old business. "Has anyone brought new business to the meeting today, get it ready to present. We have a new member with us today and we would like to make her welcome and give her a chance to speak first."

Calista stood slowly and with determination, giving each member time to take her into account.

"My father serve the company for thirty years. He has left me his legacy and stock. I have no desire to be part of this board or part of this company." She heard the intake of breath and murmuring among them.

"I will be selling my stock." She took them from her purse and handed the bundle to her lawyer. "My lawyer, Donel Ludwig, will have control of the sale and sit on the board in my place until the sale is made." She touched his shoulder showing that he had her support and approval.

"He will keep in touch with you until the time of the sale. I own fifty nine per cent of the stock and controlling interest, and all will be sold. No bids will be taken, or private sale accepted until the day of the auction. So don't contact him. I know there stocks will put the purchaser in a very high place with the company. My father wanted me to have this position but I do not desire it. I will be forming, running and teaching in my own private school."

What was she saying? Her new place was a mass of ruin. It would take months, even years to restore the castle, let alone house a school. Would she even have the finance to follow through with her dreams?

"Now if you will excuse me I will leave the meeting to you." She tapped her lawyer on the shoulder and walked out of the room.

The chairman hit the piece of wood with a shard wrap and declared the meeting adjourned until further notice. Calist was already in the hall but she heard the commotion.

Calista tried to hurry away but Kemp had taken her arm again.

"I would like very much to talk with you."

"I have nothing more to say. It's all in the hands of my lawyer."

"No, no I want to discuss other things. Could I take you to lunch?"

"I am to meet the train at two."

"Yes, yes I know. So you have said. But you do have to eat you know. I would like to take you to lunch. There is a diner at the train station. I notice you came in a taxi so this will also serve another purpose. You won't have to call a taxi." His smile didn't empress her.

Why not? She said to herself. What harm can it do? And I do have to eat. It would be a long ride before she reached Belsar and her room for the night.

Kemp held her arm until he opened the door of his car. This is so crazy she thought as he walked around the car. I don't want to lead him on or give the impression that I may be interested in anything he has to say, because I'm not. I should just get out and walk away.

There was silence for most of the way to the station.

"Why are you leaving?"

"Because I want to." she didn't have to give him an explanation, and wouldn't.

"But you have so much here."

"I have nothing here."

"Yes, you do, and could have more."

Calista didn't even answer him. If he meant she could have him. No thanks. Was this a subtle way of hitting on her again? Silence again.

"Do you know the worth of your stock?"

"Doesn't matter." She wasn't going to tell him she had no idea what it was worth, and didn't care. I'm not like you always wanting more. I have my own dreams, she thought.

"It does matter. You have controlling interest."

"My lawyer will take care of everything for me. I have what I want."

"What! A school."

"Yes, a school. That's what I want." What she had was none of his affairs.

"Where are you going?"

"Belsar." She could be as short with her answers as he was with his questions. Questions that she didn't have to answer only out of courtesy.

"Way out there?"

"Yes, way out there." This was a mistake . . . a big mistake letting him take her to lunch. She didn't want to be quizzed like a little child caught doing something in secret.

"Kemp, I have what I want. That will never change. This conversation is going no place."

"I wish I could somehow make you see what your are giving up."

"Giving up? Yes, I'm giving it up, for what I want"

"Wingate has been your home . . . your town."

She had had enough of this. "Now it is yours."

Kemp didn't say another word the rest of the trip.

Her trunk was sitting on the platform. It no longer looked like a symbol of the end. In the warm sunshine it looked like a new beginning. Yes, everything was in place. She was ready to give up this secure life and take the challenge.

Kemp raced around the car and held the door open for her, and took her elbow. What would men do if women didn't have elbows? She was needing some humor in her head to take over the confusion she was feeling. Yes, it would be safe and her life would be secure here in Wingate with Kemp. They could marry and with her stock and his they would almost own the company. Was this what Kemp was wanting? Was Kemp hitting on her for herself of her stock?

He ushered her into the diner and to a table in the corner to themselves. She ordered hot ham and cheese with a cucumber, and a bowl of vanilla ice cream.

Kemp looked astonished but said he wanted the same.

"Any thing to drink?"

"I will have raspberry ice tea." Calista wondered if Belsar would have raspberry tea. She had acquired a taste for the tangy berry flavor.

"Coffee, please." Kemp said coming to his senses and nodded to the waitress.

The smell of fried onions and philly steak made Calista wish she had ordered more. She had skipped breakfast, but her stomach was not growling because she had done without food it was because of the twisted nerves.

Being with Kemp didn't add comfort. This would soon be over, and she wouldn't have to see him again.

Calista ate everything and waited for her ice cream. She noticed Kemp had left his cucumber. Had he ordered it to impress her, because she had ordered hers.

They stood on the platform. He turned her to face him. He took her in his arms. His lips brushed hers. She backed away. What a way to start a hot love affair, she thought, and which she didn't want. Was this his way of telling her she could have him and riches. Her riches were within her own world of dreams.

"I still have to pick up my tickets." She brushed her hand across her mouth.

Write . . . soon. And always remember Wingate is your home."

She didn't turn around, answer or wave good-bye. Calista said, to herself, I will . . . I will write soon but what I write will be salable and without elbows. This time the smile spread to her face.

Chapter Two

Calista leaned back in the seat and pillowed her head until she was comfortable. She listened to the clackity clack of the train on the rails. The hypnotic sound soother her. It was as if she were going home from which she had been away for much to long, a place waiting for her. Away from Wingate and away from Kemp Maston. She had never really belonged to Wingate, nor did she desire to belong to Kemp.

She wasn't leaving home . . . home was waiting, her home. Not Clifton and Lettia's home, but her very own.

It was an agreeable day and a welcome genial, as they passed through country side filled with farmland changing into forest.

Would there still be time for her to plant a small garden? After all it was just June. In her dreams she had planted a small herb garden with a rose bush in the corner . . . a white rose. A rose bush that had haunted her dreams. She had it in her mind to make all her childhood dreams come true.

Refurbish her castle to her own liking. What would she do with the ghosts that had haunted her dreams? Were they real, waiting here in her new life? Would she be able to conquer them as she worked to make her wants become reality? Would the haunting be put into their place and pushed out of her life forever? Someone in front of her had put their window down. The sent of fresh cut grass drifted in and added to her sense of pellucid comfort.

She turned her mind lose to wonder where it would. Her hair fell down across her face and she didn't each to brush it back.

So many questions drifted in and out of her mind like the ocean current. She didn't fight them, but let them have their freedom.

Calista wondered if the property she had purchased had forests and open fields both. The pictures had just showed the castle ruins. The main castle and the bailey castle, thinking the bailey castle would be the place to start since it wasn't damaged as much as the main castle . . and it was smaller, and it would be easier to restore. The bailey castle, a place for the servants, would become her temporary home.

The real estate agent was to meet her train and take her to an inn, for the night . . . Sugar Grove Inn. Sounds like a sweet place, she smiled.

The gentle sway of the train lulled her as a mother rocks a child. She didn't want to sleep . . . sleep would just bring monstrous dreams.

Clifton and Lettia Iven, I'm not giving up your legacy, she thought, though it may seem so. I'm not leaving you. I still have your teachings . . . memories of your great love for me. I will never lose you. You will be transplanted in Belsar. You will be there with me. I can never escape you. You and your love are an eternal part of my life and myself. I couldn't escape if I tried.

She drifted back across her childhood. Mom-ree . . . mom-ree her childish voice echoed. I'm only reading, not looking for a knight. Lettia would shake her head in disdain when she read in the castle books to long.

"*You have your father's stubborn will.*" She would say. She knew it was useless to say much.

"I'm just reading mom-ree . . . just reading." But she knew I was dreaming. Dreaming of castles, knights with armor and jousting rods, dueling to win her favor. Those childhood dreams rested in the sub-concious of her mind to be dreamed again and again when her childhood over powered her waking dreams. She had no bad childhood memories all was secure and comfortable with Clifton and Lettia Iven. If she wanted to feel secure and warm all she had to do was think of them.

When my father came home from work, after one of my purchases or loan from the library, she would confront him with my childishness, my childish desires.

"When will she realize . . . knights are no more? When it is too late?"

"Our Calista will come out all right in the end." He would say and tease her until she forgot about me and her fears that I was heading for a great fall.

Mom-ree wasn't with her to soften the blow of reality now . . . neither was my energetic, hard working father. But I still had their. Strength, she convinced herself.

Dad had worked hard in the company walls to build her legacy. A legacy that I was going to sell for a repulsive, frightening dream . . . a castle dream. Would he repeat those words if he could see his Calista now? "Our Calista will come out all right in the end." How could he be so sure?

The real agent had been convincing, his letters promising, the pictures a dream come true. All that huge gray stone, weathered with the sun, wind and rain, in ruins . . . small ruins . . . but ruins non the less, ruins that could be righted.

An uneasy feeling that she had lost everything and danger was at her heels.

"Tickets . . . tickets."

Calista raised her head and searched for her ticket.

"Belsar, isn't this where you get off?"

"Yes," she said as she handed him the tickets.

"You sure were sleeping. I didn't want to wake you before." The stubby little conductor followed her to the steps. "Watch your step. Your trunk is inside the station"

"May it be left there for the night?"

"You should ask." He turned to help someone else down.

Sugar Grove Inn lived up to its name. Calista thought it should have been called Rainbow Inn. The sweet little dwelling had flower gardens and window boxes. The petunias wave a welcome to her. The lucious smell of the iris and lemon day lilies sweetened the soft breeze that washed across her face.

"Calista Iven?"

"Yes, I'm here."

"You are the one who now owns. Balthasar place?" The voice rose up from behind a low flowering shrub, slowly a head appeared.

"Yes, the pile of rocks."

"Oh, I envy you. They are much more than a pile of rocks. History, history my child. That can be made into a lovely place again. A beautiful B&B. I will help you get it started if you want to make the change."

"Is there enough business in the area to support another B&B without taking from you?" Calista had fallen into the soft voice coming from the garden.

"Oh, my yes dear." A soft smile of appreciation engulfed her face.

"We have a lot of seasonal tourists. Those that like to leave the city for a week or two. I'm booked most of the time even in winter. I would welcome having someone to help take the load off. Many are turned away."

I plan a school. What is it that smells so good?"

She stepped from behind the bush and took off her gloves. "Applesauce cake, for a snack with coffee tonight in the parlor."

"Can't wait."

"Come . . . you don't have to wait. You probably need some refreshment after that long ride."

She wouldn't hear to Calista's refusal. She washed her hands with a water hose and changed shoes. "My applesauce cake is much better hot anyway"

It melted into Calista's mouth with with the spicy tea . . . not raspberry but just as good.

"My name is Lark. Or that is what everyone calls me." She showed Calista to her room. "If you want to rest for a little while you may. Dinner will be in a couple of hours. My other guest has gone out. We won't wait for him."

Calista heard the singing coming from the area of the kitchen. No wonder she is called Lark! She stopped half way down the stairs and listened. The beauty of God's handiwork was in Lark's voice . . . such mellow tones . . . controlled.

The squeaking of the door and an interruption to the singing.

"Hey, old woman."

Calista felt the passion to rush down the steps to see who could be so rude. Not only to stop the singing but to call the lovely Lark and old woman.

"Hey, yourself old man."

Then laughter . . . intimate laughter. Clasta knew this was not the first time this conversation had taken place . . . a daily routine was her guess.

"Oh, you brought me more flowers?"

"As if YOU don't want them."

"Of course I want them, but you shouldn't have. It wasn't flowers that you went for."

"For my beautiful Lark." He teased.

"Was your trip successful?"

"Well, you just come out here and look in the truck, and see for yourself. You nosy old woman."

The door squeaked again and all was quiet. Calista needed the tenderness between them. She missed her mother and father teasing each other with tenderness. Lark and her gentleman sounded so much like them. She went to the kitchen and out the door.

"Come, Calista, see what Aaron has brought for us. This is Aaron my husband. I'm surprised you could get so many." She turned to Aaron. "Are they all guaranteed to lay?"

"Every one."

"When you need eggs, Calista just come to us. No charge. Aaron this is Calista Iven, who has bought the Balthasar place. Plans to restore it and have a school."

"It will be just like before the wars when Raliegh was living. My father loved school." Aaron said with a devilish wink of his eye.

"And your mother also. That is where they met." Lark turned to Calista with that information.

"Yes, and were expelled. They were not supposed to have a relationship or fall in love. No, sir not at that school. Raliegh was a hard man."

"Where's your car?" Aaron looked about.

"I will buy one later. Ronan Stancliff is to have me a horse and buggy tomorrow. I can use them for awhile."

"You can use my truck to take your things out."

"No need for that. I will be able to use the horse to ride around the property for a few days."

"There is a lot of territory out there to ride."

"Roman is coming out the last of the week and ride the boundary with me. He said it would take most of the day. I will need to know what is mine and not trespass."

"There is no trespassing here about, feel free to roam."

"Come, Calista, let's set the table and get dinner on."

Calista was glad Lark felt free to use her help. Aaron unloaded the truck and washed up.

They were sitting in the parlor partaking of small talk, telling Calista all they could remember about the history of the Balthasar Place. They never did call it Belthasar Castle . . . Balthasar Place, that is what it was to the town's people. Many in the town was glad someone had purchased it and had plans. They didn't care what the plans were.

"Many town's people think the place is haunted. If someone lived there again maybe the spirits could rest. Aaron and I don't think such."

"No such things as ghosts. They are only in people's minds." Aaron said shaking his head with firm understanding of what he was saying.

"Calista do you swim?"

"Yes."

"You will love woodland pool. Aaron do you remember the time we . . .?"

"Yes, of course I remember." They laughed together and Aaron took her hands in his.

"A perfect place to swim," he said.

A figure came through the door, glanced in the parlor and went up the steps. Lark and Aaron were lost in their memory and didn't notice, but Calista noticed. There was a fire in those eyes, not a burning fire, destroying fire, just a driving fire. This must be Lark's other guest, she thought.

Calista rested and almost forgot her fears. So the town's people thought the castle was haunted, but Lark and Aaron had given her new courage.

The anxious feeling began again in the little village shop the next day were she bought a few necessities. The matron didn't want to answer Calista's few questions and threw a side-ways glance to a young man that shopped in pretense. It was the same young man with the fiery eyes. He moved about getting closer with each of them. He inspected and listened with fervent attention to every word Claista said. Not another Kemp Maston, Calista wondered. Why would he be interested in me she ask herself? She thought and wondered also if he was following her. Had he left Sugar Grove Inn when she did?

She thought at one point he wished to approach with questions, but held back.

As she was leaving the matron ask. "What are you going to do with that big stone ancestral residence?" She had put emphasis on the ancestral, as if she dare anyone but a Balthasar to own it.

Her look of concern softened when Calista answered.

"I'm undecided since I haven't seen it. I'm not sure I could give an appropriate answer. I would think it could be put to good use in the community."

A bluejay twittered on a low branch of a nearby hemlock. Laughing with his shrill cry. He was laughing at me. He seemed to know Calista's dilemma. She spurred the horse on, yet the jay followed from tree to tree, chortling. Why was his clamoring haunting her so much?

Each loud cry seemed to say . . . "You've spent it all . . . you've given up your family legacy, that's what you've done. Every cent . . . all . . . all . . . all for a pile of useless rocks.

Was it the bluejay's cry or was it her ancestor's spirits screaming in her ears:

"Calista knights are no more."

She wanted to stop the cart and throw a stone at the menacing creature.

"Go . . .go your own way." She yelled aloud at the bird. "Take care of your own business. Leave me alone."

She yelled again at the bird, but it only twerped the more.

She hadn't spent every cent, and she would have the money from the sale of the stock when the auction was completed and that would be plenty . . . enough. She still had enough with her to re-establish herself. I still have this she thought. She let her eyes wonder over the cart of supplies and her trunk. Everything is not gone.

His screech seemed to echo all you have is what you carry . . . what you carry . . . what you carry with you.

Was it the bird's disturbing racket or her conscious making her feel so uneasy? She was alone in this new and unfamiliar land, yet she didn't feel alone. She had made friends with Lark and Aaron. All eyes of the past were upon her . . . judging, without sympathy, just like the jay.

Condemning the jay didn't help, she would be laughing also if she wasn't so close to the situation. One day she would laugh . . . but not now. One day it would be great laughter . . . an I told you so kind of laughter. A laughter that only she would enjoy.

Mom-ree understood her dreams but not her obsession with knights and castles.

"Most every little girl dreams, Calista. Dreams of knights in shiny armor coming to rescue them and carry her away to a castle and everlasting love."

These girls fatuous passion was for the knight not the castle. Calista's ridiculous passion was for the castle, not caring if there was a knight. Although she thought there would be one.

"I've carried my dream to far." She said these words aloud. I'm supposed to be an adult with intelligence enough to know better . . . Knights are no more . . . especially fairy tale knights . . . but castles are, castles are forever. I have lost myself many times behind stone walls of paper . . . but now my stone walls of paper are real.

Calista felt she had been up this road before . . . sometime. She sat up and looked around. When? Had it just been in her dreams? When had the jay gone? "Yes!" She had been here before. Would the ruins be familiar also? Were the Balthasar ghosts haunting her? Making all this well-known, intimate, so common to her? The castle ruins should be just around the curve. Would it be welcoming ar menacing? Would she be accepted . . .family, the Balthasar family. Now they were the Belhasar ghosts.

With zeal and wild emotions she hurried the horse on . . . going home, going home his hoofs pounded out in the gravel.

There they were . . . the ruins, set against the tall green grass. Which had just began to grow for the summer season.

There was also the knoll, the rise she stood on in her dreams. How could she have dreamed with such realistic accuracy? The knoll was calling to her, as if it had expected her arrival.

She stopped the horse just to stare . . . to remember. A tangled feeling of gladness mixed with fear overtook her. Had they really been dreams? Yes, this is home, but how could it be? I'm back, she thought, and she was connected.

Calista spurred the horse on. He turned to look at as if to say make up your mind as he stomped forward.

She rode around the castle ruins to the back and to the bailey ruins. Most of the roof was intact, there would be dry rooms inside. She promptly began to carry her things from the buggy. She had to prepare for the night even if her mind was out trying to find Lark and Aaron's woodland pool. That trek would would wait until tomorrow. She must walk up to the knoll before dark and look back at the castle ruins. Would it be as she had dreamed? Would the view be the same?

Calista was busy getting settled in for the night and dark came before she knew. She had been used to the lights of Wingate and more daylight. Would it grow dark this early every day? She had so many questions. Questions about her new beginning. She would have to make a mental note and not be caught to far from the castle at night fall. The trek to the knoll would have to wait until another day.

Chapter Three

alista had rested well, was up early and ready to explore. This morning she would go into the woods and try to find the woodland pool. The fear of danger had passed. She was here to stay and would have to make the most of it. It would be nice if she had someone to share with, even Kemp Maston. She shivered at the thought. Her mind imagined Kemp in such a place Kemp would never be at home in a rustic place.

She saddled the horse, then realized that she probably should walk. The path may not be a horse path beyond the fields. If the pond was good for swimming she would spend much of her hot days there. Or after a hard days work it would be refreshing. She would have to start the work soon on where she was going to live. But not her first day here. She was going to enjoy the day before she started to work.

Lark had said she grew up swimming in the pool almost every day. And that the Balthasar place wasn't from from it. Lark tried to tell her everything she could in the short time she was at the Inn. There would have to be another visit to the Inn and hear more stories from Lark.

Even Aaron would be more help. They had both grew up in these parts and would know much of the history. Their memories would be of help when she started to restore the castle.

They may even know some of the Balthasar ancestors. She would like to get to know the linage so it would help with the restoration.

She started out across the field toward the woods. A movement on the hillside drew her attention to the knoll, she had agreed with herself, it was the one in her dream and not menacing at all. Deer were grazing on the top near the edge of the woods. One day soon she would walk up there and look back at the castle just like she had in her dreams, but today she was wanting the coolness of the water on her feet.

When she stepped into the woods her feet disappeared in the soft moss. How green the moss was. Just like carpet she thought. Large stones stood as a wall around the path that led into the woods. Calista took off her shoes and walked along these rocks and let the misty spray of water coming down the side of the rocks cool her. It was early morning, but the sun was warm. These were not going to be ho-hum days of loneliness for her. There was much to learn, explore and work to do.

The view that opened up in the distance was more than Calista would have imagined if she had tried to make mental pictures of the pool. The beauty was breath taking. All the rocks either had moss or lichens growing on them. Many of the rocks were invisible with the coverings but you knew they were rocks. She set her shoes aside and sit down on one of the rocks at the waters edge, swinging her feet into the cool water.

Some of the frigid wintery chill was still there yet it was refreshing. The green of the trees and moss reflected into the clear water and gave it a green glow. The rushing head waters tumbled over the rocks, which were also covered with the awe-inspiring emerald tincture. Once in the pool the waters became suddenly calmed. Any disturbance at all would send ripples slipping to the pools banks only to be soothed again into a harmonious quietness reflecting the surrounding as a painted picture.

Calista was dazzled by the beauty just as Aaron and Lark must have been in their earlier years. She could see why they still held magic moments in their life of this adventurous place. A good place to build lasting moments, she thought.

A dead twisted tree reflecting in the water drew her attention and looked up to see its tangled limbs reaching to be noticed. A good place to harbor spirits she thought. Did any of the Balthasar spirits dwell there? A vine clinging to its trunk and limbs seemed to be challenging it to stand. She was just ready to defy the vine to harm the tree when she heard a splash and was drawn away to a large rock. She saw clothes hanging on a nearby branch just out of reach. A head appeared from behind the rock and looking at her with a threat for disturbing his peaceful existence. They had a stare down for sometime. Then the head spoke.

"You are trespassing!"

"Lark and Aaron said, there are no trespassers here abouts." She waited for his reaction to her words.

A transformation took over his face with the mention of their names. A softness

"Do you know them?" He demanded.

"Yes, do you?"

"Friends." Was the only word he spoke and looked at the distance between him and his clothes.

Calista stood and walked toward his few garments that hung in the branches of a small shrub.

"Don't take clothes," he almost panicked.

"I'm not taking them," she said. "I'm only putting them closer where you can reach them. Come on out and come over here and we can talk."

"Hide eyes." He demanded.

"I'm not going to watch." She reassured him.

She went back to her resting place on the rock and waited. He came toward her as if he was afraid.

"I'm not going to hurt you."

"Trespass." was the only word he spoke.

"No you are not trespassing."

"Not me . . .you."

"I'm not trespassing either. I have bought the Balthasar place." She thought she must use the name that the town's people used. He didn't come close. He seemed to be afraid.

"What's your name?"

"Idiot."

"Are you sure that is your name? Come on over here and sit on the rock with me. Let's talk."

"Lark and Aaron said new people were coming and I may have to stop coming here."

"Why would you have to stop coming? This is a lovely place."

"Lots of questions." He tilted his head to the side as if he didn't have to answer if he didn't want to. His dark brown eyes held the power for the brief time that he waited.

Calista could tell he was much older than his mind. Probably why people called him idiot. She could hear them now saying "here comes idiot" which must have given him the reason to believe this was his name. Why hadn't Lark prepared her for him. Should she be afraid of him? Lark would have said if there was danger. There was no danger image on his face.

"Who calls you idiot?"

"Everyone. That's my name."

"Well, I'm not going to call you that. So what else can I call you?"

"Lark calls me Walter. She won't call me idiot either."

"Walter it is then. Walter come on over here and sit down." It was a demand and he complied turning his back to her.

"Walter, that is a pretty name. Do you like being called idiot?"

"No!"

"Then why do you let them call you that?"

He turned and looked into her face as if he didn't understand what she was meaning. As if he would have a choice as to what he was called. There was a driving fire in his eyes.

"They just do." He dropped his head in thought.

"Again, I'm not going to call you idiot. You will always be Walter to me."

"I'll not come here again."

"And why not?"

"This is your place now. I will be trespassing." That he seemed to understand.

"I don't think you are trespassing. Come here as often as you like."

A smile cane across his face as if this pleased him very much.

"Walter where do you live?"

"You sure do have a lot of questions. I live everywhere, anywhere I want."

"Do you live in town?"

"No!"

He said it with such velocity that Calista waited for his mind to settle before going on. She waited until he spoke again.

"Sometimes Lark and Aaron let me sleep in their shed. When I'm there helping Aaron with his chores. Lark has made me a bed there. Lark is a good cook. I like it there."

Calista wondered if he ever stayed on the Belhasar grounds. His clothes looked tattered as if it was all he owned. Would she be driving him away from where he had been staying.

"Walter . . . do you ever stay here at the Belhasar place?"

His silence was more than Calista could bare. She waited.

His answer was so soft that Calista could hardly hear.

"Yes." The fear seemed to take its place on his face again.

"Lark and Aaron are very nice." Calista said it in a tone as if she were speaking to a child.

"Yes . . . very nice." He admitted with arrogance of love. "Very nice."

"Why don't you come back to the castle with me and we will have some lunch."

"Castle?"

"The Belhasar place."

"Castle?" He questioned again.

"Yes, my place."

"Ruins."

"Yes but they are dry." She wondered if he stayed in the castle ruins and would now have no place to go. Surely he must have someone . . . family. She started to go but Walter just sit still.

"Are you hungry?"

He didn't turn to look at her fore some time. Then he nodded his head.

"Lark always knows when I'm hungry."

"I bet she does. Lunch today won't be anything like Lark would fix but it will take away the hunger."

"She will send Aaron out to find me and he brings food. Lark always knows."

"Well, come on let's go to the ruins and see if there is anything there."

"Not unless you brought it, there ain't," he smiled at her for the first time with an agreement and movement.

Calista walked in front of Walter leading the way back to the ruins. She noticed he was leaving the path to gather dried branches into a bundle on his arm. When they were in the open field he bound around her and she thought he was going to run off from her. He went some distance and laid down his bundle of twigs, and came running back to her. He grabbed her by the hand and almost pulled her up the embankment toward the knoll.

"Walter will show you something."

"Wait there is no hurry."

He slowed down to a walk but didn't let go of her hand. When they were in the place where the deer were grazing earlier he stopped and turned her around to face the ruins and the point beyond. She almost gasp with the image before her. Just like in her dreams.

"Look at the mist rise."

"Walter it is beautiful."

"Walter lives there on the crags most of the time."

"Where do you go when it is raining or cold?"

He turned away from her and let go of her hand. Alright he is not answering so she knew. He lived in the ruins. Somewhere in the ruins. She had taken his hiding place.

"Look at the sky!"

"It's so blue."

"My favorite color. Sometimes the waters are just as blue. But most of the time they are covered with mist, just like today."

"Do you not get wet from the mist, sleeping under the jutted rocks?"

"Jutted rocks? There is a cave. Not wet at all."

So he didn't stay in the ruins he had a place of his own. And she would never make him leave it.

"Come let's go eat."

He started to bound down the knoll in front of her but stopped and let her catch up with him. He picked up his bundle of branches and walked on beside her.

"What is your favorite food?"

"Lark's applesauce cake."

"Yum, it is good. I had some the other night when I stayed at the Inn."

"You stayed with Lark? She has lots of people stay there, and she always makes applesauce cake. I don't go when she has people."

"And I bet she sends some out to you."

"Most of the time if there is any left."

"Today is your lucky day."

"Lucky day?"

"Yes, that is when you get what you want."

"All, Walters days are lucky days then. I have what I want every day."

She gave Walter the applesauce cake while she made sandwiches. It was a pleasure to see him enjoy the sweetness. Yes, and she would enjoy having Walter near to keep her company. He would be someone to share with when the Balhasar ghosts got the best of her mind. She noticed Walter staring out at the road.

"You have people . . . I will go."

"You are not going until you eat."

"Idiot will . . . Walter will go."

She was glad that he had accepted the fact that he was no longer idiot. At least when she was around. In no time she would have him forgetting the word altogether.

When Calista looked out the road she expected to see Aaron coming. To her surprise it was the young man with the firey eyes that had been staying at the Inn.

Chapter Four

Calista didn't raise from the beam where she and Walter had sit to eat. She let the new people, as Walter had called him, walk up to her. He had a backpack. Was he just here for the day to explore? One of the tourists? He was walking slow and looking around as he came toward her.

"Hello, I'm Dugan Balhasar."

"Calisa Iven and this is Walter. She didn't give a greeting, just Calista Iven. Walter had sit up straighter when she said his name.

He extended his hand to her. Her pause made him start to draw back but she stretched her hand and met his. Why had he come now? The place was sold. She hoped she didn't let her feelings show. Should she welcome him or turn him away?

The fire was gone from his eyes and there was only amiability there. How could he be so friendly when she had bought his place before he had the chance? Lark had told her he was in the village for that purpose. She should have taken this as a warning. Maybe he proposed to offer a purchase price to her. Not likely, for Balhasar wasn't for sale, and she would let him know this from the first.

"Do you mind if I look around? I've never been here before. It's just as lovely as mother and father said."

She couldn't deny him a visit to his paternal family home. Just as if she ever went back to Wingate and the company of her legacy, she wouldn't want to be turned away. Why he waited so long to make an appearance?

"No I don't mind. Look all you like."

He took off his pack and laid it down beside the beam she and Walter were were sitting on and started around the ruins. Calista watched as he went out of sight toward the tower. She was planning to explore the tower herself this afternoon.

Walter kept looking at her with questions in his eyes. Then he walked away. She leaned back against the stone and let the warm sun seep in. She began to rehearse an argument in her mind if he should offer a price. This was her childhood dreams come true and she wouldn't part with it, under no circumstances. Belhasar was hers. Dugan Balhasar was to late.

She stood and walked to where she could see the tower. Dugan was going across the concrete arch bridge that connected the tower to the castle. He pushed the door open and was swinging his arms fighting cob webs. He faded out of sight but still she watched for some time.

He came into view again at the very top of the tower. He stepped out on the narrow balustrade testing every step to see if it would support his weight as he walked all the way around. When he stumbled once Calista thought this is just what I need.

An injury and so far from town with only a horse and cart. But if he fell from the tower it would be more than an injury, maybe death.

He stopped before interring the door. He was looking at the sea. He raised his hand and gave a wave. Could he see Walter on the rocks? Was Walter watching to see if she may need him? She looked toward the sea but the horizon hid the jutting cliffs.

She waited as he again faded from view. She was still watching when he came back across the bridge and came toward her.

"I will stay in the tower."

"The tower?"

"Yes, it will be out of your way. I will refurbish it at my own expense."

"Lark tells me you are going to restore the place and have a school. You will need teachers. Will some of your teachers stay on the grounds? I would think that there would not be talk if a teacher stayed in the tower."

"That's right I'm going to have a school. But there is so much work to do before it will be a school and ready for teachers. And none of your affair she thought. She hadn't thought about teachers and where they would stay or if there would be other classes. She had only thought about herself and teaching writing. Did she want such a pushy demanding teacher in her school? She would be the one to hire them after all.

"I'm an artist. I teach art. I would like to teach here. Raliegh Belthasar, my great grandfather had a school here. He taught art. My desire is to follow in his footsteps. Be, the artist and teacher as he was."

"It is a long way from being a school"

"Not so far away as you might think."

"There is much work to be done before it can be opened as a school."

"Again, not so far away as you might think. I have some ideas that I would like to share with your creative mind. You must have an inventive mind to see a school in these ruins, and so do I. I see the school." He said arrogantly, knowing that it could be done. Had he formed the same plans in his thinking? "Again not so far away as you might think."

She could see the irritation of him having to repeat himself and demanding his way. Well, Dugan Balhasar get to work. What was she thinking? This stranger to be a part of her school. Could he be trusted?

She couldn't help but think he was just bidding his time to ask to buy Balhasar and again bring it back to it's rightful existence and ownership. This was not going to happen. She was determined as any Balhasar could be.

He went on talking and sharing his ideas and never once offered to purchase the place.

"I will take the tower. Have my studio on the top floor where there is plenty of light and the classroom on the ground floor. There is plenty of room for living quarters between. I'll stay the night, fight away the spider webs and go for the rest of my things tomorrow. There isn't much to do to the tower to make it ready, not much damage at all."

"The possibility of a school isn't that close."

"I will have to stay on the grounds to do the work. I can take care of myself. I will be out of your way unless you need my help with something."

He didn't give her time to decide. How could She refuse? She did want her school soon. And with him doing part of the work on the tower, it would be a good start. Maybe her dreams were not so far away. She wanted to get to teaching writing as soon as possible and with help it could be near.

"Have you seen the view from the tower?"

"No, after all this is my first day here."

"Yes, I know, and it is my first day also. Come, I'll go with you and show you the tower. I have already done away with the cob webs. There won't be much work there. It was spared the destruction."

He picked up his pack letting her know the decision had been made. He was staying. He turned and walked toward the tower and Calista followed. She had began to feel the weight of the Balthasar ancestors on her heart. What a responsibility there was before her to restore the school just as Raliegh Balhasar's dreams had been. Just maybe Dugan knew more than he was telling about all he knew about the past school.

Lark had said Raliegh was successful with his school. Maybe she had trusted Lark and Aaron to much. What if they hadn't warned her just to see how strong she was. All their tales just a farce to see how far she would take this dream. Wanted her to fail and be gone again so Dugan could have his ancestral home. But here he was offering suggestions and help to do the restoration. Did they really believe there were still treasures here on the grounds?

"Have you heard that the art work of Balhasar may still be here on the grounds?" He asked.

"Yes." She didn't want to get into the information she had heard and where she had got the information.

"Is that why you bought Belhasar?"

"No, My will is for a restored school."

"The art work itself is quite a legacy. If all my information is correct. And I wouldn't think my family would have reason to lie to me."

She dropped behind him not wanting him to be able to read her expressions. She wanted to ask him if the art work was why he was here also, but she refrained from doing so. Let him prove himself.

"Come on, race you to the top," he challenged.

The walk form Belsar must have given him energy. Calista thought as she took the challenge and raced in front of him. The cool waters of the woodland pool had also given her energy. But she was sure when she stepped out on the balustrade he had let her win.

She could feel him standing behind her waiting for her to sober from the awe-inspiring view. He touched her lightly on the shoulder. Would he push her, she thought. She didn't know the Balhasars. Were they an evil lot? He stood for some time with his hand on her shoulder. Had he come to get rid of her so he could have the grounds?

"You know," he spoke softly, "if the mist would roll away I bet you could see right into tomorrow."

Somehow she thought this could be so. Had she seen into tomorrow when began to dream about the ruins, when the realtor sent the pictures of Balthasar?

Tomorrow.

A movement on the rocks drew her attention to the jutting rocks and to Walter standing looking with vigilance, watching and tilting his head to the side as if he was also listening.

If Dugan was evil and pushed her, Walter would see. Even with his childish mind Calista felt safe having him watching. Could his infantile mind be broken under pressure? Would he make a good witness? Had this really been Dugan's first time here? Was Walter watching because he was aware of danger and her safety? Didn't other senses develop when one was impaired? She had always been told this.

"There are so many landscapes scenes to paint here. It is an artists paradise."

"Do you teach other than classroom studies?"

"Oh, yes, my class will roam all over the grounds and paint what is an attraction to them. This is what makes great art. But yes, there will be classroom studies as well."

Calista raised her hand and waved to Walter. It seemed as a small signal for him to keep watch. She was trusting Walter, her new friend. Calista was trying to depend on her diplomacy while she analyzed her safety,

Dugan solved the problem between them with his remarks and with lack of malicious intent.

"Your desire and my desire are the same for the ruins. I just want to be a part of the restoration. Be true to the Balhasar name. Don't pass judgment on me Calista."

"I'm not."

"Yes, you are afraid. I'm not dangerous. Thoughts are racing through your head so fast I can hear them." He chuckled.

Had he caught her wave as a signal to Walter?

"That isn't funny." she said and stepped back into the tower. Dugan followed and began to give her the details of what his studio would be like. The lighting would be perfect all times of the day because of so many windows. He would need very little artificial light.

"I'm so glad that most of this tower room is windows. I will be able to move my easel to face all directions. If I had all my things here today I would try to paint the sunset on the misty waters. I may even put the child in the painting."

"Walter isn't a child." If Dugan stayed here it wouldn't take long for him to understand what Calista had understood from the first meeting, that Walter was not a child but much older than his mind.

He waved his hands in front of her face to be sure he had her attention. She was lost in thought of being here just one day and already had to new friends one she trusted and the other would have to be proven.

"I want to paint the castle ruins before you start the restoration. I want them just as they are. I will take pictures tomorrow so you can start your work. Where did you stay your first night here?"

"In the bailey castle. It was much dryer and not damaged so much." It was none of his business where she had stayed. She had answered to quick. Calista was getting annoyed with all his chatter and questions. This was her place. She felt that he was taking over. She had not told him he could stay or to be on his way so he must have read that to mean he could start his planning.

"Just like the tower. Really it isn't going to be as much work as it looks from the beginning."

"To know where to start . . .' Calista was thinking out loud.

Dugan followed her and kept chatting what he was going to do here and what he would put over there.

"Just look, there could be fifteen easels set up here in this room easily. A teacher and fourteen students. It would definitely pay for itself."

They stepped into the room he planned to be the classroom.

"I will stock paints, brushes and canvases here so the students may purchase them . . . Other supplies can be stocked later. Storage spaces can be built under the stair well."

The last words she heard as she walked out and left him talking to himself and planning his classroom. How long would he chatter before he discovered she was gone? She wanted to think. Things were moving to fast for her to grasp. This was just her first day. Already she had a new friend in Walter and Dugan, someone she didn't trust moving into the tower. He planned to be a part of Balhasar and the school. Yes, she had to, do some sorting in her mind and emotions. She would not let Walter down she wanted to spend some time with him. He needed a friend.

Chapter Five

C alista had fought with her thoughts most of the night, yet she woke rested. Her dreams had stopped since she arrived at Balthasar. Her mother's words had also stopped but she listened for them every day.

She couldn't help but watch in the direction of the tower, even though there had been no movement all morning. Was Dugan gone? He had said he would go for the rest of his things today. He must have gone early, for she had missed him leaving. Where did he have to go? To many questions attacked her thoughts. Did he have to go to Belsar or . . . where? How long would he be gone? Why should she care? There was work to do.

Walter hadn't been around either. Had he taken Walter with him? She couldn't picture Walter going off with Dugan, a stranger.

She wanted to start on some of the ruins but Dugan had ask her to wait until he had taken some pictures. She went back into the bailey ruins and began to make her living quarters more comfortable.

She wanted to work on the main castle and get her living quarters moved over there. She convinced herself that Dugan wouldn't want inside pictures,besides she had moved into the bailey castle and it was her private place for now, no pictures would be taken. After all the bailey castle was just a temporary place. Calista wanted to start on the main castle and get moved over to the space she had picked out for herself.

She finished up the work and walked over to the main castle. There was a lot of planning to be done. She walked through an open hole in the ruins onto the main floor. A door would have to be made first. Her privacy was the most important thing for her right now with Walter and Dugan on the grounds.

Walking around in the ball room she heard a car approach. Could it be Dugan coming back? She waited. She didn't want to seem anxious to have him back.

"Calista? Cal . . . lis . . .ta."

That wasn't Dugan or Walter's voice. Kemp Maston! Why hadn't she gone to the woodland pool today or took the horse for a ride around the fields. What was Kemp Maston doing here? Still she waited. His voice called out her name again a little louder. Just go away Kemp. She had nothing to say to him. She would go out and send him on his way.

"What are you doing here?" She sounded irritated.

"You call this home . . . and a school? It is just a pile of ruined stones. Calista what are you thinking?

"Yes, it is home. And will soon be a school."

"There can be nothing made out of all these piles of rubble. You must have lost your senses. Come on back home with me. I will take care of you. This is not the place for you."

"There can be and will be." She stood her ground very forceful.

"You are out of your mind. I came here to take you back to Wingate."

"I'm not going anywhere."

She knew in her heart that Kemp Maston didn't have it within him to persuade her to leave. She was here to stay. Was he looking to get her and her stock. So determined, that he would come this far.

"Why are you wasting your time and mine? I have lots of work to do."

"I'm not leaving until you are packed and your things in the car. I'm taking you back to Wingate with me. I have always wanted you to be mine. Remember high school? I tried to tell you then."

"High school is past and gone, we are no longer kids. Don't be so foolish. I'm not going anywhere."

"Yes you are." His determination was strong.

Calista felt a light pressure of a hand on her shoulder. Kemp looked beyond her face.

"Is there trouble here?"

Dugan's tone let her know he would take up the fight for her. Had she been so busy with her work that she had missed his return?"

"No, no problem. He was just leaving." She said without looking around. She was thankful that Dugan was back. She kept looking into Kemp's disgusted eyes.

"No problem at all."

She wondered if she should introduce Dugan. Doing the proper thing would be to introduce him.

"Dugan this is Kemp Maston, from Wingate. Kemp this is Dugan Balthasar."

Kemp stood for a long time staring at them. Realizing he had lost, with a disgusted grunt he turned and walked back to his car and was gone. Dugan kept his hand on her shoulder until he was out of sight.

"Thanks," she said with an actual feeling of gratitude.

"Any time," he said without stopping. "I will take the pictures as soon as the sun comes to this side of the ruins and you can start on your work." He replied and took his hand from her shoulder and walked back across the bridge to his tower.

Calista went back into the castle and went up the steps to where she could see the tower. Dugan was unloading his car and taking his belongings into the tower. She wanted to go help but was afraid she would seem to forward.

"Calista."

"Walter, where have you been all morning?"

"Watching the mist rise from the sea. Come let me show you."

He looked out the window and watched Dugan toting a heavy object.

"Should we go help?"

Walter looked to her for advice. If Walter went with her she could help without seeming impertinent. They walked together and pitched into the work. When she entered into the space set aside for a classroom she saw that Dugan had already set up his painting board with paper and some etching.

It was of the ruins. When had he done this etching? Had he done it from memory? Had he been back long enough to do the sketching?

With the work done she knew they should go.

"Come now Calista, let me show you the sea."

"Where will we go to observe?"

"To the Knoll, hurry."

Walter was almost in a run. She followed as fast as she could. He was used to these hills and she was used to the city streets. It was a struggle to keep up with him. How long would it take for her to get used to taking the knoll without stopping?

"Come Calista."

"Walter what is the hurry?"

"You know how fast the mist can come in again."

This was her second day here. Of course she didn't know about the mist.

"No, Walter I don't. I have only been here for a short time."

"Well the sea is very temperamental. That is what Aaron calls it . . . temperamental. The mist can rise in a moment. I don't want you to miss the view as it begins to slide in."

"I'm going to be here forever now Walter."

She had seen the mist from the tower yesterday with Dugan, but it was already over the waters. She didn't want to ruin Walters excitement.

"I want to be with you when yo see for the first time."

"Okay . . . okay."

When they reached the knoll Walter turned her around and watched her face.

"Isn't it beautiful?"

"Yes, it is magnificent. Walter it is so awesome. Look how it rolls."

He smiled at her with pleasure.

"I have enjoyed this for so long. It is good to share."

"And I am glad to share it with you."

Calista could see the mountain range that followed the edge of the waters. It was truly a work of art. She was going to have many subjects to write about using this setting. There could be mystery, romance and lots of description with an environment like this. Yes, this is truly where she wanted to be.

"What is he doing?"

Dugan had moved his painting board to the front of the ruins and was taking pictures.

"He is taking pictures. He wants to paint the ruins just as they are before we start the restoration.

"Restoration? You mean build it back like it was long ago. Lark said it was beautiful. She has pictures."

"Yes, I plan to restore the castle and have a school."

"Walter will have to go."

"No Walter you will not have to go. Your home is here. You will never have to leave it."

"When people come Walter will have to go."

"No."

"People will come. I will be called idiot again. I like being Walter."

"You will always be Walter. I will not allow people to call you idiot again."

"You can't stop them."

"Yes I can and will. Those who would call you idiot will be the ones to go."

He stood shaking his head so hard that Calista thought he would do himself harm. His hair flew from side to side.

"No . . . no you don't understand. You can't stop them."

Clasta wanted him to understand. His life had changed when she walked into it. He would never be called idiot again. She wanted to take him in her arms and rock him like the little child that he was. She took his hand and put her arm around him and stood silent until he stopped shaking.

"You will always be welcome and you will always be Walter."

He looked at her with credulous eyes. He was inclined to believe her, but the doubt was still present. She waited and waited . . . hoping he could feel the desire within her to make his life better.

After a long silence he said, "How will you stop them? . . . fight."

"If I have to. Has Dugan ever called you idiot?"

"No."

"Have I ever called you idiot?"

"No."

"Dugan and I will be the leaders and others will follow. When they see us calling you Walter. They will call you Walter also."

"Will the people from town come?"

"I don't know who the students will be or who the teachers will be. That isn't import now. But you will not be called idiot."

"Dugan will be one of the teachers. He teaches art."

"Art?"

"Walter have you ever gone to school?"

"Idiots don't go to school." He spoke with sordid words as if she should know this. It would be so stupid to think an idiot went to school.

"You are not an idiot. Art is making pictures with paint. Dugan will paint the sea, the mist, the ruins and make it look just like a picture."

"Won't be as pretty."

"It will be pretty, but never like the real thing." she agreed.

"Is he painting the ruins now?"

"He is taking pictures and sketching. He wanted to have pictures of the ruins as they are now. Then when we finish the restoration he will paint the castle just as it was in the beginning."

"Won't be as pretty. Will he paint my rocks?"

"We will have to wait and see."

"My rocks are pretty."

"Yes they are."

As if Walter realized what he had said he turned to her.

"They are not my rocks anymore are they? They are yours."

"You can always call the rocks yours Walter. Nothing is going to change for you. Nothing important that is. And it is important that you think of the rocks as yours."

"Will he let me watch him sketch?"

"We can go down and see."

Walter watched in awe as Dugan began to sketch the ruins He tilted his head one way and then the other.

She left them and went into the bailey castle and made some sandwiches. When she returned Walter didn't look her way he was so absorbed with the action of Dugan's hands and pencil. She spread out the cloth and arranged the sandwiches in three groups.

"Time to eat."

Walter didn't move until Dugan put down his pencil and sat himself on the ground in front of the spread.

Days seemed to fly for Calista. Every morning when she would go out to work on the ruins Walter was already there moving heavy beams and doing what he thought she would want done.

One morning Walter wasn't there. Calista looked at the sky. A storm was coming. The dark heavy clouds began to pelt the ground with cold rain. Calista ran toward the rocks as the wind took up the furry of the storm.

"Walter . . . Walter where are you?"

"I'm in here."

His voice came through the hollow opening in the rocks.

"What are you doing out in this storm?"

"I came to see about you."

"The wind will blow you into the sea. You haven't been in storms like the ones we have here on the sea."

He grabbed her hand and pulled her into the opening as if he knew she was in danger. She followed him into the opening and was surprised at the large room in the rocks. Walter had taken some of the beams and made seats on one side of the room. He had a bed made on the floor with moss and leaves. A raggety blanket lay on top of the moss and leaves.

"Is this where you live?"

"Yes, see how dry it is? It never gets wet no matter how hard the storm. We are safe."

Calista sat down and listened to the storm. The thunder rolled over the ground, right out to the waters and disappeared into the mist. She tensed as lightening lit up the cave. She would not be able to go back to the castle until the storm was over. She was sure Walter would not even let her try.

"There is nothing to be afraid of. The storm can't get us here. Walter has seen many storms come and go and he has been safe."

"Will the tower be safe?"

"Long time the tower has been there." He smiled. "Dugan can take care of himself. You have me to look after you."

"Dugan . . . will . . ."

"Safe don't worry."

Calista realized she was worried. Walter began to hum a soothing tune. She leaned back against the rocks and closed her eyes. She felt more comfort that she had since her father and mother's death. Her mother had always held her, rocked and hummed to her when a storm came. She would like to be out on the knoll. Would this storm be the same as the one in her dreams?

Chapter Six

*W*alter had gone and Calista was fighting with a rough beam, ready to give up for the day. She looked up to see Dugan only steps away holding a tray of food.

"What a captivating carpenter." He smiled at her with a soft look. Her heart leaped in her chest. It had been keeping up this pace every time she seen him working about the tower.

"Not so," she chided. "Unlike you which seems to have no trouble at all."

"Hungry?"

"Dugan that is your painting board!" She was surprised he would use it for anything else but painting.

"Makes a nice picnic table. . . yes?" He smiled at her again and set it down on some of the ruins she had been working on.

"Yes . . . yes." She answered both questions. "Yes I'm hungry and yes it makes a good table. But I didn't think . . ."

He waved, not letting her finish the sentence.

"Yes," she laughed aloud.

"You have been at it all day, miss carpenter. Is there a rush?"

"Of course," she hoped she sounded urgent. "Winter is only six months away."

"Six months and you are worried?"

"Not really," she dropped her head and took the plate he offered. "I would like to get as much done as I can before then. I don't know what the winter here will be like. I don't know what to expect,"

"Neither do I. But I plan to make that a change if you will let me."

"The tower is yours as long as you want."

"Thanks. I sure hope you won't get tired of me and send me packing."

"Dugan, . . . will you tell me what you know about the Balhasars in the evenings when we finish our work for the day? I would think your family has told you many things. I would like to get started on writing the history. I want to do the restoration . . . perfect. I need to do much more research before I do much on the castle."

"I'll come over this evening after I get things cleaned up. Is that too soon?"

"No, I would like to get started as soon as I can."

When Calista came out of the shower, Dugan had come in and built a fire.

"The evenings here are a little chilly, aren't they?"

"I'm used to cool evenings. Wingate evenings were cool. We made a fire every evening just to take the chill off."

"I'm used to the warm southern evenings in the city." He arranged the chairs until they faced each other. Motioned her to sit down. "Where do we start?"

"From the beginning."

"I'm afraid that Genesis has already done that for us." His smile didn't relax her pounding heart.

"Are there books in print that I could read?"

"I want to know everything you know, every thing you've been told, everything you have heard and everything that I can read. Lark and Aaron have told me a few things they know. I'm sure they could tell me more. Is there history anywhere? Anything that I can get and read?"

"What do you want to know about the Balhasars?" His voice changed to a solemn timbre.

"I want to know everything you know, everything you've been told, everything thing you have heard and everything I can read. Is there history anywhere? Did your family have pictures?"

"The art work that Raleigh hid here on the grounds is the only pictures that I know of. The library in Belsar has a book called called, 'Belhasar in the Beginning'. The book tells of my great grandfather's battles and his reward from the king which was Balhasar Castle. The king gave the name in a presentation celebration. It was a great celebration with all the town's people present."

"That would be an interesting book to read." She would be sure to find it.

"I know some history is over emphasized by the teller of the tales before it is written down. Once it is written word it is very seldom changed. Many truths are eliminated, many of them exaggerated. I would rater know what is told by the family and passed down from generation to generation. How do you know I will not add to or embellish the truth just to make the Belhasar name look good."

"I don't. But I am willing to listen." She knew she would take any over polished quotes and make up her own mind if they were truth. She wasn't afraid to ask others that may know.

"Just, tell . . .let me be the judge of what I will believe."

Dugan got up and walked over to the fireplace, leaned on the mantle, put is foot upon the hearth and laid his head on him arm.

"Sounds fair." He came back and sit down and continued.

"I know you will be able to find microfiche in town. It would be a time consuming and a project for winter days. They would probably be available in the library or newspaper office. Knowing the year would be a big help. Maybe you could find an older reporter that would remember. I wanted to do this but time and distance didn't allow it. I do know the library has films of the drama class plays. You could watch them and learn about the drama class. All this would be interesting to look into. I plan to see some of the films."

"If I'm going to restore the castle as it was in the beginning I must research every source I can."

"It will be impossible to restore it to the original."

"Why so?"

"It would be inconceivable to think it would be original unless the art work is found and hung in their proper place. Then and only then will it become the original Belhasar Castle. Or do you plan a name change to Iven Castle?"

How dare he ask such a question.

"No, I do not plan to change the name unless the living Belhasars object. Why do you think I am researching the initial beginning?"

The questioning look on his face almost gave her fear. Did he know where the paintings were? Did he know she would never find them?

"I don't think any living Belhasar will object."

"If they are on the grounds, do you not think I will find them?" She had determined no stone would be left unturned that could be moved. Every inch would be searched.

"Many have tried."

She got up from her chair and walked over to him as close as she dared. She did not want to give away what her heart felt when she was close to him.

"Many have given up to easily. I don't give up so easily. I have set to the end to restore this legacy, with or without help. Now will you tell me what you know?" She threw her hands in the air almost striking the mantle.

"Raleigh Balshar, my great grandfather was a slave to his own will. He would be proud to have someone with the same soulful will as he, himself. I wish he knew there was one like you so determined and searching to restore the place."

OK, so he had accepted the fact that she was a willful and determined soul, with a mission. If he only knew, she thought. She had struggled with her desires to own a castle for twenty five years. Or at least most of that twenty five years. Her desire had been to restore this castle from the first sight of the pictures that Ronan had sent. She still had the same determination. She had not given up on owning her own castle, having her school and now she had her own. *It would be restored,* just as she had wanted.

"Being so willful is what made Raleigh a noble and regal knight in the king's army. He won many battles and deserved the land and the castle that was built for him. It was his will to win, if it be in battle of war or of love. With a new castle he must have a wife and children, was his thinking. That is the way it was with him. When he saw and sought after Silvia Wellton. It became a battle for him, so strong that it almost lead to self destruction to win her. He wanted her in his arms and in his home. There could be no other."

Were all the Balhasars so determined, she thought. Would Dugan be a strong knight and soldier for what he wanted? In love and in war. Would the castle treasures mean war.

"Silvia was promised to another. Raleigh met her at one of the town balls. He fell for her at first sight. Raleigh and her met secretly and fell deeply in love. Their love and passion became surrender for them both."

What would it be, to be loved so? Calista was fascinated with wonderment if this kind of love would ever come her way? Was she really in her dreams wanting a knight?

"No longer wanting their love to be secret they fought to be together.

Silvia was as determined as Raleigh. Their love could no longer be kept hidden with secret meetings. They wanted to be together, more than life itself.

When her promised husband found out Silvia had been unfaithful he became unstrung. He struck out wildly, with a strength that only a rejected man can.

All Raleigh's soul knew was that his desire cried out to win. And the battle began.

The battle would have been until death if the rejected lover hadn't realized his loss and backed out of the picture never to be seen again. If he had not the consequences would have been great for him because of the king's love for his knight and lord, Raleigh Balhasar."

Calista was so engrossed with the story telling. When had she left his side and sit back down? She was aware she could not find such family passion in history books. Would she ever be so lucky as Silvia, she ask herself again? Was there a knight out there for her somewhere? To fill her castle with love. Were all these dreams she had wasted her time on been for nothing? Would her knight fight for her love as Raleigh had for Silvia? Who would he fight, she had no one. The desire to be wanted had never been so strong.

"Go on." She needed to get her mind from herself and Dugan and get back to the Balhasar story.

"My great grandfather was born in October. The beginning of the end. Just as October is the ending of summer. October with all its color.

"Raleigh's knighthood battles were over. The season turned into color and so it was with him, he turned to his colors and art work. When he settled into being lord of the castle instead of a warrior he sought with the same fervent passion for his dreams to become an artist."

Was her mother right all along? Did everyone have dreams and seek them to the end? Would Dugan in his story telling reveal his own dreams?

"I'm afraid that I have also inherited this passion for the pigments of color. I have studied art in many schools. But most of it comes from the desire within."

Yes, Dugan was going to insert himself into the Balhasar stories. Was he also telling her that he was doomed with the same soulful will and would stop at nothing to get what he wanted? He wanted Belthasar castle for himself and came here to purchase it. She had beat him only by days.

"Raleigh Balthasar again, Please." She didn't want to give him time to change his mind or lose the feeling of the moment. The air was full of static for the story and she didn't want it to end.

The fire snapped and warmth filled the room with a pine smell that added to the magic spell.

"Raleigh's moods, temper and outbreaks caused much havoc in his early paintings. He would lock himself away for days just to paint. Before a master piece could be rescued he would destroy it, instead of covering or repainting the color. Just because one color didn't please him. He drove himself forth with a fire few people have."

Oh, yes she had seen the same fire in Dugan's eyes the first night she saw him. A challenging and driving fire. Driving to possess what he wanted and what he planned.

"He was called lazy many times because they thought he refused to sign his paintings . . . but since he was a lover of secrets each painting carried his signature hidden somewhere within the painting. His paintings could not be plagiarized because to the normal eye the signature could not be found until pointed out. He kept a ledger where each signature was hidden."

Had the ledger also been hidden with the artifacts of the castle? Would she find it when she found the paintings.

"Some artists do that. But usually it can be sighted after an extensive search. They must have been hidden well for him to keep a ledger."

"There were just so many paintings that he wanted to make sure. The ledger wasn't for him. It was for Silvia and the family when he was gone.

"If a gallery contacted him about a painting that might be his, he would tell them where to look and if the signature wasn't there, they knew it was a fake and not a Balthasar painting."

"Did he ever stop a sale because of a fake?"

"Oh yes many times. There was so much in Raleigh's work . . . every lucrative. He was sought after. He loved his work and his art was displayed in many galleries and homes. But his best pieces were hung right here in his and Silvia's home. Silvia and the family loved his work as much as he did."

"I have seen the peg holes and some of the pieces of pegs still protruding from the stone wall. I thought when I recover the paintings those holes and pegs will help me determine just where the paintings hung."

"That will help you know where a painting hung but it will not tell you what painting was there."

"Is the ledger among the hidden treasures?"

"I'm not sure. My mother didn't tell me of the history until she was old and she had forgotten much of the tales that were passed down. Just like most of us we are interested in our own wants, dreams and plans to fuss with family history. Why should we be interested in family ghosts?"

When I started painting was when she opened up to me and started telling me these stories."

"But now you are interested."

"Yes, very much so. I would like to see the paintings, find one of his and see how much of his talent I possess."

"If they hung in galleries and homes would it be so hard to find one, so you could use it to compare?"

"The wars destroyed and ruined much. I haven't found one as yet but I still look. If his best pieces were here that is what I want to compare with. It would be hard to derive if it was a true Balthasar painting without knowing where the signature was hidden."

"Then do you think the ledger is hidden with the paintings?"

"I'm hoping for that to be so."

"But there was fire in some of the castle."

"When the wars came the treasures of the castle were concealed in a private place that only Raleigh and Silvia knew. The hiding place had been built by Raleigh himself. Even the servants didn't know. That is why they have never been found. The secret place died with them."

"I will find them and they will find their proper places again. Where was Raleigh's studio?"

"In the tower."

Was that why Dugan had chose the tower? Did he think the treasures were there? A fear was tossed into Calista's heart. Dugan surely must believe the hiding place was in the tower.

"No more than the fires damaged the castle they could still be right here in the castle walls. Raleigh was as good at hiding his treasures as he was his signature."

Was he telling her they could be in the castle to side track her from the real hiding place? Did he want to keep her busy searching the ruins while he searched the tower? Calista was ready to confront Dugan with a question of truth.

"Have you come back here to claim the paintings? To hunt for them?"

"They would not be mine even if I found them. They went with the sale. The treasures of Belthasar would be yours . . . who ever the finder is. I just want to see them. To know they are safe."

"Do you really believe this?" And with the determination you have to restore I will fight with you to see that this happens."

"*Knights are no more . . . Calista . . . your dreams will take you on a path you do not wish to go.*" Her mothers words came loud and clear.

Was this just more of Dugan's lies?

The fire had burned low and the room had darkened. Please momree don't send a warning now. Not tonight. I have relished the stories of Raleigh. Was Dugan as secretive as his heirs? Would he feed her this line to distract her from her true goal? Would he take her prize away if he found them? Did he have his own castle that he wanted to store the family legacy in? Would she lose the Iven legacy and the Belthasar legacy both? He must have a clue that they are hidden in the tower. Was that why he had demanded the tower for his? Had he really convinced himself the treasures, if found, would be hers? Would she be in a fight to death with him?

"If reincarnation is possible I think you have inherited Raleigh's will, his drive to accomplish what you want. He has led you to restore his legacy."

Was this why she had felt the strong feeling of belonging? The very first day she had been at home . . . even in the ruins.

"But Dugan, don't you think these traits would have been kept in the family line?"

"No, I don't. Spirits have no boundaries. You have been sent here by providence . . . fate . . . what ever you want to call it. That is why I accept the fact that the sale was made before I had the chance for the purchase. Raleigh had been working with you from your birth. Your drive to own was real . . . meant to be."

"It has been very strong!"

"I can see that. I feel that Raleigh's spirit has given me the talent to paint, to teach painting, to fulfill his dreams of Belthasar art. That is why I want to compare my work with his. How much like his is my work? What direction will I have to go to carry the Balthasar name with pride? I want my legacy to carry on. The are legacy of the Belthasars."

"What! Do you think Raleigh is working with both of us?"

"That's possible."

Dugan punched up the fire and put on another log. Waited for the fire to catch and the room began to glow again. Calista just sat and let the words make themselves at home in her mind. Could Raleight truly be a part of this restoration? If his spirit was working, yes, she would find the paintings, all the restoration depended on them. Raleigh would want the paintings in the correct places and without the ledger or records it would be an impossible trek. She would have to have something to build on. A beginning. Could she trust Dugan enough to let him be a part of the restoration? Did Dugan know enough of the family history to be of any help? All of his information was only hear say and passed down from generation to generation and was deluded with added to and left out information.

"Raleigh and Silvia had years of trouble bringing children into the world. Silvia became pregnant every two years but never carried a baby to full term. She did it to six months once, but she lost them in the third and fourth months. When she had carried the one for six months they were hopeful."

Dugan paused and waited.

"It was still born and a girl. They would have welcomed a girl if she was just healthy, even though Raleigh was heartbroken for a boy. They felt this was their punishment for going against the promise of Silvia to another. So you can see when she finally carried Buryl to full term, they were very proud."

Calista could remember how her father and mother had doted their love on her since she had been an only child. The Iven's had wanted more children but it didn't happen.

"Buryl began to bring disgrace to the Balthasar name. Raleigh and Silvia were at their wits end trying to control him. It is getting late and I think we should leave Buryl for another time."

Calista was pleased that he wanted to wait. She had enough to meditate on for now. She had to put all this information into its place in her thoughts and mind. She wanted to dwell on what Dugan had told her about Raleigh working with her from birth to restore the ruins.

Dugan built up the fire again and left her to her dreams.

Chapter Seven

When Calista came out the next morning a truck was unloading lumber in front of the ruins. How had she slept through all the noise? The truck finished and drove around to the tower and began unloading the rest of the load.

"What is going on?" She questioned Dugan.

"You need a door before you can move over here. Walter and I are going to build one today."

"Yeah!" Said Walter smiling at her confidently. "Build one."

"Yes, you can trust us. We really do know what we are doing."

"No doubt. I will stay out of your way."

They both looked thankful. Calista turned and walked back into the bailey castle. She hummed around doing some work feeling a little nostalgia not only for her mother and father but for the ghosts of the Balthasar family.

Could the spirit of Raleigh really be helping Dugan and her in the restoration? She couldn't get this question out of her mind. She had struggled with the idea of spirits during the night. Did she really believe in them?

She put on her bathing suit under her clothes and started for the woodland pool. She needed some thinking time. Were the ghosts real? She had to settle this in her mind before long. If they were real she had to believe didn't she? She would have to trust in the underlying feelings. The feelings of ghosts being about.

When Dugan and Walter began to do the hammering she knew she wouldn't be able to stay away. She would want to help or interfere in some way. If they were going to build a door, yes, she should stay out of the way? Would the woodland pool be far enough away?

It was such a warm day. The mist was gone from the waters and the view was breath taking. She walked slowly along the path. Had Raleigh Balthasar walked the same path? Had he and Silvia held hands as they walked together? This had been their kingdom. She became silent waiting for them to speak to her. But only her mother's words rang in her heart. *Calista knights are no more.* Over and over she heard these words ringing in her heart. Words with power and feeling. Her mother's feeling of doom. This feeling was bringing on will-o-wisp desire. Yet she was not an ignorant day dreamer as her mother had thought. Life was real. She had her dream here in these ruins. The ruins were tangible. Something she could see and touch . . . and existing. Could she make her dreams come true with these ruins?

She wasn't a lazy sloth. She didn't mind hard work. She wanted the school, the restoration and she wanted to be a success. Prove to herself and her mother that it wasn't just day dreaming. It was her life long desire and it was here and it was real. She would have to make it happen. It had worked out so far so why was she having these doubts now? You can't build on doubts she told herself. How many days of doubt would come before she had accomplished her dream? So much work had already been done.

Raleigh had been a true knight. Why didn't he speak as her mother had. Why couldn't she hear his words?

Dugan had said that Raleigh and Silvia had thought their punishment for going against the rules was Buryl. What would her punishment be for following a dream? Would it be failure?

"No." She screamed aloud. No, she would not let that happen. She would fight with all the Iven strength within her. Her father had been a success and she would prove she could do the same.

She took of her clothes and jumped into the cool waters of the woodland pool. It will happen . . . it will happen . . . it will happen she told herself with each stroke across the pool. She would shake these doubts. It will happen. I'm not a weakling and a quitter.

She stepped out of the cool water and sit on her sitting stone in the warm sunshine. The doubts were still there. Her bathing suit began to dry. I will go into Belsar, establish a permanent address, no more Wingate, no more Kemp Maston, no more company matters with her father's legacy.

She would let Donel know she wanted to sell the stock and sell it now. Her life was here no matter what turn of events happened. The catastrophe would be hers to bare and make the most of. There would be no failure. I won't accept failure. Dreams do come true. There is plenty to work with.

Peace began to come slowly. She knew who she was and what she wanted. She was secure within herself when she put her clothes back on and started back toward the ruins. They would not be ruins long. She not only had herself, she had Walter and Dugan to help. In Wingate she would have only Kemp Maston. She shuttered at the thought.

Coming out of the woods into the field the knoll began to drag her to it. The knoll of her dreams. Is this the beginning of reality? It was the beginning of her dream. She was always standing on the knoll looking at the castle.

When she reached the summit she turned toward the ruins. Walter and Dugan had not seen her. She watched them for some time. They had the door almost to completion. Had she been in the pool that long?

They were hanging the door when she started down the embankment. It seemed that something pushed her down and was holding her to the ground. A weight pressed on her back. A heavy feeling of holding her there for a purpose. She began to claw at the earth hoping to pull herself free. The ground began to give under her hands. A small corner of a brass object became visible. She pulled at the earth but it had grown tight to the object. The weight was gone from her back and she ran toward ruins.

"What's the hurry?"

"I have found something."

She sounded urgent. She grabbed the shovel and started back up the incline. Walter and Dugan were holding the door in place and could not go after her.

When she found the corner of the object she began to dig away the earth with care.

"A marker!" She said aloud and began to dig with more fervent excitement. **'Iola Balthasar'.** Who could Iola Balthasar be? She wished Dugan had told her more. Iola had not been mentioned. Was this one of Raleigh and Silvia's daughters? Dugan had not spoke of a daughter. Only the one that was still born. Why was she buried here alone? Was there a family cemetery here? Would she find more graves on the knoll? Did Dugan know about the grave? She brushed away the dirt and roots. No, this was not a child. She had lived to be twenty eight. Her own age. Who then . . . who? Was this the Balthasar apparition of her dreams? The gauzy ghost that stood and watched? Was it her that held her to the ground? Did she want to be found?

Calista could hardly wait until Dugan was story telling again. Would he know who she was?

She looked at the ruins. Walter was coming up the slope. Dugan was motioning her to come.

"You've got to come see." Walter said excitedly.

"I'm coming."

He took her hand and pulled her faster.

"You've got to see the door. It is a good one."

"I can see that."

They had built a cross buck door. Large black metal hinges held it in place.

"Look."

Walter ran to the door and opened the slide to reveal a peep hole.

"You can slide this and know when I'm here. And open the door to let me in or Dugan in. If you don't want who is at the door you can tell them to go away."

"Yes I can. I will always let you in Walter . . . and Dugan," she added.

Walter opened and closed the door a few times to show her how it worked. "It's a good door. We are going to paint it gray just like the weathered rocks. Dugan said so."

"What did you find?" Dugan was looking from her to the knoll.

"A grave marker. Iola Balthasar."

"Buryl's wife."

With his silence she knew he would wait until the tales of Buryl Belthasar to explain more.

"I'm going into Belsar."

"Here take my car." He handed her the keys.

"There's no need."

"Yes, there is. It is getting late. You do drive don't you?"

"Yes I drive." Her irritation was evident. Dugan just smiled and motioned her to go.

"Of course I drive."

The road to Belsar wasn't as long in a car. She was glad Dugan had let her have the car. The nostalgia and thinking time tired her more than she wanted to admit.

She stopped by Sugar Grove Inn first.

"You have mail." Lark turned to go into the parlor. Calista followed.

"Lark do you mind if I ask questions?"

"Of course not. I hear Dugan Balthasar came out to the ruins."

61

"Yes, he came the first day. He is rebuilding the tower. He has put his studio on the top floor and classrooms on the ground floor. He wants to teach art when the school opens. He is doing a lot of work."

"His great grandfather, Raleigh taught art in the very same tower and had his studio was on the glassed top floor. How is the restoration coming?"

We are getting it cleaned up pretty good. Dugan is putting the ruins on canvas as they were before we started the restoration. Walter and Dugan built a door today and it is really nice."

"Oh so you have met Walter already?"

"Yes I met him the second day I was there. He was skinny dipping in the woodland pool. Do you know who he is? Does he have family?"

"He has no family that he knows of. He don't even remember his mother. I think you should let this information work its self out."

"He told me his name was idiot at first but I pressed him to tell me what his real name was. He said Walter is what you and Aaron call him. He doesn't know what his last name is. So it is a mystery to me."

"Some of the town's people called him idiot. I never would. He is much older than his mind as you have already found out."

"Do you know what his last name is?"

"Again this information should work its self out. The name on his birth certificate is Hart . . . Walter Hart. His mother's maiden name was Hart. He is a bastard child."

"Buryl's?"

"No not Buryls. Ask no more it will come about in time. How did you find out about Buryl."

"Dugan has been telling me history of Balthasar family, in the evenings when our work is done. Buryl is as far as he has got with his stories."

Lark handed her the mail with a questioned look on her face. It was from Donel Ludwig. Did Lark think it was from a lover? It was written on personal stationery.

"I'm sorry my mail came here. It is the last place Donel knew I was going to be. I came into Belsar today to establish me an address at the post. Walter said you always knew when he was hungry. He enjoyed the applesauce cake I took with me. It was such a joy to watch him devour the sweetness. He is doing well, Dugan and I are feeding him."

"It is his favorite. I have two baked you will take one back with you and Aaron has you some eggs. I have looked after him since Lareina passed away. It was so hard for him at first. He didn't know what to do with himself. He has made him a home at Balthasar. I told him he may have to leave since the property was sold. Aaron lets him help some around here when we don't have guests."

"He loves it there and he thinks you and Aaron are the best. He will always be at home at Balthasar."

"I'm glad to hear that. It would upset him something awful to have to leave."

"Has he always lived in the cave?"

"No he lived in the small castle in the winter. In the room with fireplace so he could keep warm. He is good at gathering wood . . . seems to always have enough. So you are still sticking with the plans to have a school?"

"Dugan thinks we should have more than just writing classes as I had planed at first. He will teach art. He has said there was drama, music and other classes when Raleigh directed the school. He would like to have it restored as it was in the beginning and so would I."

"It would be nice to see the ruins like they were when the Balthasar's lived there. It brought in people to Belsar. If you are going to the post, it is getting late. Go establish your address and come back to get the things to take home with you. Aaron did well on his purchase of chickens. We have eggs running out of our baskets."

Calista hurried to the post but took time to read Donel's letter before going in. It was full of questions. Are you happy there? When do you want to sell? The company is getting yancy. They don't like being held at bay. Will you come back to Wingate for the sale? What is your new address?

She went into the post and established her address, bought a post card and wrote only a few lines. The new address, sell now, I won't be there for the sale, handle it.

On her way back to Sugar Grove Inn she stopped and did a few chores and then to a car lot. Why not do it all while she was in town.

A salesman came out of the office looking at his watch. Lark had told her it was getting late. Did Belsar close down by the clock? Not like in the city at all.

"Interested in a vehicle?"

"Yes."

"Trade in?"

"No just a purchase."

"Nice trade in. Just what my daughter has been looking for."

"Not mine."

Calista could see he was irritated by having to stay overtime.

"What is the price on that pick up truck over there?

"Nice vehicle."

He took a book out of his pocket and thumbed through it. She was sure he knew the price without looking it up.

Again he said, "nice vehicle and quoted her a price. Good condition, lots of extras."

"Since it is getting late I'll be back tomorrow."

"Don't open until ten."

Back at Sugar Grove Inn, Calista smelled the applesauce cake before she got out of the car.

Here are the eggs and cake. You and Dugan can share it too. You might want to keep it with you. Walter has an appetite big enough to eat it all at once."

Chapter Eight

The evenings had been very busy and Dugan hadn't come to continue his stories. Calista had so many questions. He and Walter had been hammering and banging around in the tower for the past few days until after dark. She busied herself in the main castle getting her apartment ready for the move. Staying away from them had been hard for her. How long would Dugan keep her waiting before he came again and told her about Iola Balthasar? He surely must know the identity was baring on her mind. He had to see the excitement the day she found the grave.

Ronan came and rode the boundary with her. She had taken the horse and buggy back that day and bought her truck. This took her mind from Iola for a few hours. She had ask questions of him. She had to get all the information she could find. He came to Belsar as a realtor to sell repossed properties and collecting debts due the town. He knew nothing of the Balthasars.

Were Lark and Aaron the only ones that knew anything about them and the school? The lady in the general store seemed to know Dugan. The day she was shopping there she could tell the ladies loyalties were for the Balthasars. That was evident when she wouldn't answer her questions. Why was those in Belsar so set against her? She was afraid she had collected all the information from Lark that she was going to get. Lark seemed so distant the day she was in Belsar. Was she still wanting her to fail so Dugan could have the property? Was Dugan spreading falsehoods about. Where was the undermining happening? Lark had talked about Dugan being at Balthasar. How would she know if he hadn't told her? Did this little town know everything that was going on? Many times in this situation the town would know before the one involved knew what was going to happen to them next.

Calista wasn't objecting or criticizing Lark or the town. It was just the way it was sometimes. She would work her way upstage and become part of the drama. She wouldn't become outraged and let her dignity suffer. She wouldn't be humiliated by their gossip and bluntness. No she would be part of what would happen from this day on. Create her own drama.

The gossip and theatrical living could be used to her advantage. Her name would be out there in the foreground every time the Balthasar property was mentioned. When she began to look for teachers and students for her school it would be on the lips of everyone. They would come to see. What an advantage this would be. Even the tourists would carry on the tales of the school when it opened.

She would plan tours, open house, orientations and yes. She would be a good director. She would write and direct her own plays. And the school and Balthasar would not play a skimpy part in this drama.

She heard a noise at the front of the castle and walked down the steps. Someone was banging on the door. Who had cosed the door? She had left it open for the breeze. She swung open the door.

"That isn't what you are supposed to do. What if it wasn't me."

The eager enthusiasm in Walter's voice let her know he was testing her. Walter backed up and the door was closed between them and the pounding came again. Calista slid open the door and peeped out.

"Walter is that you?"

It sounded like child's play to her but she complied to his wishes.

"Yes it is me. Let me in."

"I thought you and Dugan were working on the tower?"

"He is painting. Said the light was just right."

"Oh."

"Painters are moody aren't they?"

"What is he painting?"

"Don't know. He wouldn't let me see. He said it was a surprise for someone. He was looking at the knoll. Can he paint the Knoll? Make it look real?"

"I would say he can paint anything he wants to."

"Why does he close the door and lock himself in?"

"I think his great grandfather used to do the same thing. Carrying on a family tradition.

"Just not right. I wanted to watch."

"Yes painters are moody but then so are other professionals. I get moody when I am working on a story. If the manuscript isn't going the way I want it to."

"Professionals?"

"People who do just one thing. It is called their profession."

"But Dugan don't do just one thing. He can build doors and hammer nails. He is making the tower look nice."

"Profession is what you make a living at. Dugan will sell his work for money."

"What if it is good and pretty and he don't want to sell for money. Sometimes you just don't want to sell for money. I know."

"If you are through helping Dugan, would you like to help me carry some of my things over here?"

"That would keep me busy."

Walter had already grown accustom to having people around. She wouldn't have any trouble keeping him busy for the afternoon. He felt important when he was helping.

"What is that?"

"A computer."

Calista was setting the computer on the table she had found in one of the classrooms and cleaned it for this purpose.

"What do computers do?"

"I will show you as soon as we get telephone lines. They are a lot of fun. You can find anything on them."

"Rocks?'

"Of course rocks."

"I find rocks and keep them. I have some really pretty ones. Sometimes I gather shells too."

"Some time you can show them to me."

"Don't you ever want to buy them for I won't sell them for money. Money means nothing. I remember where I found all of them."

"When we get phone lines I will show rocks on the screen here. Maybe we can find some of your rocks in the pictures."

"Not my rocks. I have them hid. No one knows where, not even Aaron. He wanted to sell some of them for me one day. So I hid them were he couldn't find them."

"He wouldn't sell them unless you said he could."

"I wont ever say that. You will have to promise you won't want to sell them."

"I wouldn't sell your rocks Walter."

"You have to promise. Then I will show you,"

"I promise."

"Cross your heart. Lark tells me this really means a promise."

Calista placed her arms across her chest and said, "Cross my heart. Is that alright?"

"That makes it a real promise," Walter smiled contented. "Now sometime I will show you."

They stayed busy all afternoon. Calista felt like she was teaching a small child as she answered his curious questions. He caught on well and remembered most of the important things. She wondered if she could ask him questions about ghosts without upsetting him. Deciding against it she pushed it from her mind.

"You need bookshelves."

"Yes I do. Maybe when you and Dugan get finished with the tower, you and him can help me build some."

"When you want to build them I will help. Dugan can do without me. You are first."

"We will let Dugan help too."

"You are first. And you make me happy. You gave me a place to live. And Walter is never hungry now."

"And you make me happy. You have shared your excitement and your fears of Balthasar with me. You have even told me how the mist can come and go. And you kept me safe from the storm."

Walter leaned back with pride and the biggest smile she had ever seen.

"It isn't always over the water. It is most of the time but sometimes it stands on the knoll."

"On the knoll?"

"Yes . . . It just stands there and looks at the ruins."

"What stands there Walter?"

"The mist. Some people think it is ghosts. Aaron said that Balthasar is haunted. That means ghosts live here."

Walter stood proud as he told her what he thought was something she didn't know. Now he was teaching her.

"When you see the mist on the knoll, will you come and get me? I would like to see if I can see it too."

"It is there most mornings. Most of the time it is when the mist is gone from the waters."

"I would like to see it. Walter are you afraid of the ghosts?

"Oh! No they are of dead people. Dead people can't hurt you."

"Who are the dead people?"

"I guess it could be anyone. The people in town used to tell my mother and me it was the Balthasars haunting the ruins to keep people away from their treasures."

Walter was placing the books on the floor with the spines up so you could read the titles. She hadn't even told him to do it that way. He wasn't an idiot. He was just untaught and maybe a little slow.

"Walter would you like to read one of the books?"

"Walter can't read."

"Would you like for me to read one to you?"

"I don't know."

"Come on sit down. I'll start this book and if you don't like it we will stop."

Calista chose one of her childhood books that was her favorite. She began to read and Walter sat mystified. It was hard for her to keep her eyes on the words, she wanted to watch Walter.

She read about a little boy chasing bugs and was planning to put them in little sister's sandwich to get even with her for getting him in trouble with their mother. The story went on how the boy cooked the bugs so they wouldn't make his sister sick. He didn't want make her sick, he just wanted to get even.

"I don't have a sister. I don't have anyone since my mom died."

"I don't have a sister or a brother either. I don't have anyone either."

"Do you not have a mom?"

"No my mom and dad both died in a car wreck."

"My mom got cancer and she couldn't get better no matter what I did for her."

"It isn't your fault Walter. There isn't anything anyone can do with cancer."

"I tried real hard. Do you think the reason we like each other is because we don't have a brother, sister or mom? Dugan has a sister. He told me."

"We have each other Walter."

". . . and Dugan?"

"Yes, and Dugan."

"He is nice even if he is moody. I guess sometimes I'm moody too."

Calista patted him on the arm and started reading another book. This one about a boy chasing a zebra wanting it for a horse. Walter listened intently and would laugh when the boy failed with all his tricks to catch the zebra. They both laughed when they looked up and Dugan was standing in the room.

"I wondered what happened to you."

"You were moody and painting. I will not be helping you when Calista starts to build bookshelves. I will be helping her."

"Oh, may I get in on the building of the bookshelves too?"

"You will have to ask Calista. They will have to be what she wants."

"Why don't you ask her you seem to have more sway with her than I do. Do you think she will be bossy? And try to get in the way."

"I don't know."

"We do have some boards left. Do you think we could talk Calista into taking them off our hands and use them for the shelves?"

"Bookshelves."

"OK bookshelves."

Walter's lightening flash look in her direction was evident that he wanted her to take the boards.

"Will you?"

"I don't see why not. Since I do need the bookshelves."

"I will be over this evening to go on with the Balthasar history."

"Iola?"

"We will start with Buryl and see where we go."

Chapter Nine

That evening Dugan came. Calista couldn't read his face he seemed troubled. Was this going to be hard for Dugan? Questions, questions she had so many questions but she waited on Dugan to began.

"I will dwell on Buryl first, we will get to Iola, his wife at a later time. The story should be told as it happened."

Calista wanted to have the story in order but she had found the grave marker and was anxious for the mystery of Iola's marker and why she was burried alone and not in the Balthasar cemetery.

"Buryl Balthasar . . ."

Dugan's pause was so long that Calista was afraid he was going to make up his tale. Was Dugan just a good fantasy story teller? She had heard that story telling was an art in itself. See who could divulge the greatest lie that would still be believable . . . but false. Many places had a yearly contest for such stories with prizes. Had Dugan been around and entered such facades? Had he just been making all these tales up?

Entertaining her. She believed in the passions and secrets of Raleigh and Silvia in her heart. Or did she just want to believe, were these little things she felt in her very being, doubts? Were there really art work and treasures hidden here on the grounds or in the castle ruins, or buried in some disclaimed place that no one had ever found. Could they be buried in the Balthasar cemetery unmarked?

She needed more history that was not biased by family fantasy. Most families believed theirs to be the best and have the only way of rightful living. It was always the outsiders that seemed to sight all the flaws. Yes, Dugan would have to be proven real. Was this man standing before her really Dugan Balthasar? Was he a bounty hunter, a treasure chaser . . . a good liar that had done his research and done it well. And she was letting him live here without knowing.

A treasure chaser would stop at nothing to find the treasures they were seeking. And they would lie naturally without thought, knowing in their heart that there was no way to trace the truth. The lies seemed to fill their mouth at all times just waiting to be spoken, almost as if they pushed the lips out in a pout waiting to be uttered. Why was it so easy for lies to come forth without effort?

She wanted to believe. She didn't want to be tricked into being a fool. Had all her childhood dreams come to this? To be carried away into a fantasy world of lies. Is this what her mother meant when she said this dream would take her on paths that she wouldn't want to go? Yes, she would find other sources for the Balthasar stories. Dugan would be proven to her satisfaction.

These feelings she was having for Dugan could and would be pushed aside. She was a pro at pushing what she didn't want in her life into an empty void to be recalled if she ever wished to do so. And If Dugan proved to be fake she could easily forget him and leave him pushed into her void.

"Buryl Balthasar."

He said again as if he didn't want to reveal this part of the Balthasar lineage. After all Buryl was his grandfather.

"Buryl is another story altogether. Where should I start with Buryl?

As you have said in the beginning. Mother and I have always wondered if it was because he was born to Raleigh and Silvia's later years that made him what he was. It was like he had a dual personality . . . good against evil and both in control. He had a double fire driving him . . .at times gentle . . . yet he would explode into a rage that became almost violent within the same moment Seemed as if he was controlled by some evil force that could appear at any moment."

Was Dugan like this? She couldn't help but think he was. All the Balthasar's hates, loves, fears and wants, all past ancestry contained in this prison cell of Dugan Balthasar. Would he be dangerous if crossed? Not given what he wanted, if he didn't have unvarnished control. If he found the treasures would he be violent to have them. A flow of strength welled up within her. She would fight for them because she wanted the Balthasar castle restored to its own identity and she would stop at nothing to get what she wanted. Maybe Dugan was right, she did have some of Raleigh passion.

"Buryl thought his parents only lived to make his life miserable. They tried to hold a tight fist to his wild antics. Tough love is what it was called. He would over rule their warnings and laws to do what he pleased even as a small child. He knew the consequences yet trespass."

Dugan paused again and turned away. This was uncomfortable for him so she waited silently.

"This is very difficult for me because he was my grandfather.

Household laws along with the laws of the land were pushed aside when it was his will to do something. He would say yes when the answer should be no, when he was asked questions. Buryl was almost an outlaw with his recklessness. Maybe I should say he **was** an outlaw and never had to pay the price that is carried with being a transgressor."

Dugan also knew the consequences if he trespassed, she thought. If he found the Balthasar treasures would he try to whisk them away? Would he be like Buryl his grandfather try and try hard to get his will?

"Buryl means a server of wine to the lord of the castle. Was it Raleigh's wish to make him a machine? To serve his dreams? That is what parents do sometimes. The dreams he had of what Buryl should be. Where he should stand in the Balthasar family. Was Buryl's rebellion to the rules of Balthasar, to prove he was his own person, and wanted his freedom?"

Dugan left the fire and came over to where Calista sat. He sat in the chair facing her.

"You are a lot like that. If you have a dream you go after that dream. This is why you are here. Your will is to have what you want."

So he did see the fight in her and knew she would stand true to what was hers.

"Yes, I have wanted to own a castle since I was a small child. In my mind I have always owned it." She wondered had she given her parents the same heartaches, Buryl had given?

"Now it is no longer in your mind, it is real. Are you satisfied? What are your real plans for your castle? Has your dreams been fulfilled?"

"I have many plans for Balthasar." she deliberately didn't answer the fulfillment question. Her plans had changed since Dugan came to stay. To add art to the plans for the school and other classes also.

"Plans, yes, but are you going to turn them into reality?"

"Yes!"

Another time Calista would have been offended at these words but it was her choice not to be lured into her response at this time. Did he think her as a reckless renegade as Buryl must have been. She knew her stubborn childhood dreams had brought her this far. Dugan picked the story up as if he had never stopped.

"All the ancestral ruthlessness seemed to hold Buryl captive. When you trace the Balthasars back you can far back beyond Raleigh there were skeletons in the path of the Balthasar lineage. The family tree squeaked with bones. Skeletons they tried to hide, but floods of reality uncovered then and added more shame since they were of hidden quality,"

"Buryl was ruthless but not hard hearted. He could be as gentle as he could be rough.

Being wild seemed to be a competitive game for him, possessing his every waking moments. He was not a born leader yet he had many that tried to follow and imitate him. When he saw something he wanted he took it. He didn't consider it a tiresome conflict if it became a challenge. Win he would. He was the same with women he didn't care if she belonged to someone else, nothing would stop him, pheasant or nobility.

She would be his for a time and many times it was almost the end for him, just like Raleigh when he wanted Silvia. Buryl would blaspheme God, family, laws and even the elements. He wouldn't let it rain on his parade."

Dugan started to take Calista's hands but saw her mine pull away, so he stood and went back to the fire. Turned back and stood looking at her. The smell of fire mixed with the smell of man drifted down over Calista' head and took over every breath she drew into her nose. The smell of man was over powering. She had always liked the smell of shave colones and lotions of men. No! She would not let this man draw her to him. He was not her knight, yet she could yield to him easily. So easily she seemed to be frightened by the feelings that welled up inside her when he was around.

Calista became uncomfortable with the stare. He had the advantage. His back was to the fire therefore his face was shadowed. She wanted to read that face, know his thoughts as he spun these Balthasar stories.

Dugan must have felt the tenseness because he left the telling of Buryl for another time.

"Raleigh had a successful school here. The castle is built for classrooms. Raleigh had drama, dance, music and he himself taught art. Each year the drama, dance and music students would put on a performance for the town's people. All would come to the joyous festivities and the castle would be crowded for days. It was a fall performance when all the color of nature was present. There is a large amphitheater on the grounds somewhere. I haven't had the time to search it out yet. Have you"

"No, I was not aware of its existence."

"What you have planned is writing and art . . . right?"

"Yes and you brought the art to light."

"Yes, I did."

"I had never thought of the other arts as being a part of Balthasar. I just wanted to use my talent and studies to teach what is dear to me, writing. I can see writing is not enough. The other arts should be included. This will take much more planning."

"Is the reason you accepted my art, you were more on the line of writing-illustrating? Calista, I'm not an illustrator. I am an artist. I teach art not commercial illustrations. It is not likely one of my students would ever become an illustrator. You will have to look else where for an illustrator."

"I was not planning on using you."

"No openly but I'm sure it has crossed your mind."

"Not ever." She said with force. "I would never agree to something just so I could use someone."

Calista saw the clash of wills for the first time and felt them creeping in to devour them both. A shiver came up her spine but went unattended. She refused to let him see he had gotten to her. She would get what she wanted and he would fight to the death for what he was. No, he was not her knight.

"Calista, knights are no more."

"Oh!" Oh my she thought. She shuttered inside. Was her mother alive in him? Lettia Iven alive in Dugan? Had she sent him to keep her safe . . . to warn her? To keep her away from her dream? Were the spirits really living her and pushing them on?

Well they were failing because Dugan wanted the restoration as much as she did. Or was that just another of his falsehoods? Was it also to distract her . . .to scare her away. Oh, my how would she ever keep calm now? Her mother's words still echoed about the room in Dugan's voice. *See Calista you are never going to be rid of my warnings.* She gathered her nerves and gave a deep sigh and hoped her voice didn't reflect her temper.

"I'm not looking for a knight."

"Yes, you are . . . you really are."

"No."

"Yes and by the was your friend Kemp Maston isn't a knight either." Had he read her mind again?

"He's not my friend."

"Then why was he here?"

He put his fisted hands on his hips as if to say now explain that.

She didn't have to tell him why Kemp Maston was here. That he was really wanting her legacy. Her father's legacy that was left to her. That he worked for the company which she held the controlling stocks. It was none of his business. And was Dugan here for the same reason, for the legacy that she had bought? The Balthasar legacy.

She wanted to yell at him, oh, shut up, just shut up and go step in a cow pile. I'll have my stories. I'll have my illustrators. I'll have my school. And if it takes dance, drama and music to go with her writing to be a success she would have that too. She would put Balthasar back to the original so be it. **I will** have my school. I can make plans, organize, find teachers and students. I'm not a stupid dreamer.

"One of Raleigh's rules for his school was that love couldn't bloom between student-student, teacher-teacher, or teacher-student. If they found love they both had to be dismissed or expelled. Any form they had too leave Balthasar. Buryl may have had a hand in that rule with all his love antics."

"That was a cruel contract to be ruled by." Was that a look of pleasure hidden on his shadowed face? Did he agree with her statement?

"Was it?"

"Yes."

"Can you be your best when you are lost in thoughts of love?"

"Yes, I would think you could."

"Maybe we should leave Buryl for another time."

He walked away swiftly, back to his tower she hoped. Back to his high and lofty tower. But for her, emptiness had filled the room.

She put another log on the fire, took her pencil and notebook and sat down to write.

Writing wouldn't come . . . no thought . . . blank.

She turned the page and her pencil went to the center of the page and wrote 'Drama' as if on its own. Calista ripped out the page wadded it and tossed it in the fire.

Again she wrote in the center of the page . . . 'Drama' as if it was a heading, waiting for titles, sub-titles. She made a small a: and wrote teacher, a small b: and wrote students. Yet another page, 'Music' a small a: teacher, small b: students. She didn't stop until she had headings for each . . . drama, music, dance, writing and art. It was as if the pencil gave her back control when it was finished . . . yes, and writing she wrote the word again. She wrote it with defiance. After she made the heading and wrote her name on the line as teacher. Then she turned to a blank page and wrote Balthasar School of Fine Arts, Calista Iven: director. She turned back to the heading 'Art' and on the line she had placed a small a: She wrote the name Dugan Balthasar. Yes, the school would be back to the original with a Balthasar teaching art.

Don't just step into a cow pile, Dugan Balthasar, may it hit you on the head and into your face with it. Childish . . . maybe . . . maybe not.

Kemp isn't a knight but neither are you . . . a liar . . . a teller of stories, no Dugan you are no knight.

Calista began to analyze Dugan from the first evening in Sugar Grove Inn, when he had come in the door and looked at her with such fire in his eyes. She slid back in the chair, rested her head on the back and stared into the fire, watching it snap and make sparks into the air.

You'd think she would just close her eyes and let his presence in the room fade, but she didn't . . . couldn't. She kept the thoughts of him and the smell of him in her mind as she closed her eyes.

Neither of them would take orders from the other. Were they concentrating all their flaming energies toward determining who would win in this battle of wills. These mutual challenges tossed back and forth to each other until one gave up and walked away . . . or war. Would there ever be an attainable harmony between them? Her answer now was NO. Had destiny designed them to be together even if it was in war? They were both independent and would rather war than learn from their mistakes as to have some well meaning person council them of their faults.

Was he full of false pride? If she ask that question of him, she must also ask the same question of herself. She began to analyze him even deeper and compared him to herself. Everyone had their shortcomings didn't they? Even, she, her self. Did he think he had no flaws, could do no wrong, everything he did or said was right, and at all times sound, sensible and wise? She must also look at herself to analyze if she felt the same way. This war was not fair.

With the pride of her verbal right hook she time and time again hit. Still her explosive temper only fanned the fires in Dugan's eyes the more as his image wouldn't fade. She has analyzed not only him but herself and she was ready for battle. She would be ready when the fight came to be real. Her pride wasn't wounded, tarnished or even gone. Yes, she had her pride and nothing in Dugan Balthasar could ever wear it away. She was an Iven and of good lineage.

Her life had never before had lies in it. She was having trouble believing what Dugan was telling her could be lies. She wanted to believe so deeply and he sounded so believable. Should she just pat the peacock on the back and let him hang himself? She smiled within.

Yet the room was so empty . . . hollow . . . lacking . . . void . . . ever since he left.

She knew if she let him stay in the tower, have his art studio there, teach his students, she would have to give in and work with him. She would be the director and must learn to get along with all teachers.

She would get used to having him near but not as a knight. Dugan would never be her knight. Had he spoken truth only when he voiced the words that she was looking for a knight? Had all these childhoods dreams really been for a knight? Love welled up in her heart and mind. Yes, she would have her knight and she would be the one to chose the right one in time. Somewhere . . . sometime he would come riding into her kingdom and be her helpmate. Was she daydreaming? She pushed these thought aside and let her mind roam.

Calista put another log on the fire and sat back down and got comfortable. In her mind she walked from the bailey castle over to the main castle. She began to plan where she would start on the restoration. Have the castle ready when she found the treasures, have the castle ready for them to take their rightful places.

When the time came she would find them. Raleigh's spirit would lead her to them. She rubbed her hands across the stone walls, peg holes and she felt the peaceful feeling of being home and alive with energy to preform the duties that stood before her.

She stood before the great fireplace and saw Raleigh and Silvia's image there. She had them in her mind already, What they had looked like. It would be the place to put them if their likeness was hidden in the painted treasures. She wished with all her strength that there would be painting of each one of the family that existed before the destruction. She wished mostly for the image of Buryl. She wanted to look into his eyes and see how much of herself would be there, or would he be the image of Dugan? Would she be able to see his reckless strength and draw from it, feel his strength to have what she wanted. Would these feelings dampen the spirit of Raleigh? Would he still help her with the restoration? Had Buryl brought so many heartaches that Raleigh would not want Buryl's image around?

She sat up with a start . . . of course he would want Buryl there after all he was his son and of the Balthasar lineage.

With all of Buryl's capers, tricks and follies in his life Raleigh would want him to have his rightful place in the restoration, in the Balthasar castle. She couldn't imagine a parent that wouldn't want their child in the family history. Dugan has included him in his stories. Buryl would not be left out.

Sleep came and so did Calista's dreams. The dreams had taken a change. They had taken on the Balthasar family. Images of the Baltshasar faces and she stood among them.

Chapter Ten

Calista couldn't get Buryl out of her mind for days. With each piece she moved of the castle ruins, she wondered was it something Buryl had touched? What of these ruins were a part of him? What part of the castle apartments belonged to him and Iola? Was his strength and wildness still a part of the ruins? Each day she had more and more questions. Did he sit here or there to make plans for his antics. Plan his reckless rebellions.

Yes, it was Raleigh and Silvia's castle but there was Buryl. Even if they didn't like it he had his own rule. He couldn't be pushed aside. Was she falling into a fantasy for Buryl. A ghost?" Would there never be reality in her life? Had her mother seen the truth as it was being played out in her life now? Had mom-ree been right all along? Was she traveling a road that would bring demise to her and her will to succeed? Would she reach a point of no return . . . no turning back?

The Balthasar family wouldn't leave her thoughts alone. They were always pushing her on. She wouldn't be at peace until she learned all she could about Buryl and his family. Dugan's family. In all this pilgrimage where would Dugan fit in?

When she began her writings would she have enough information to write and bring up to date the Balthasar history? That was the plans for her first manuscript. If so, she would make Buryl into a hero.

His life couldn't have been all bad. A knight, a ghostly hero knight. Buryl a knight. What would Dugan think of the knight she had picked out, his own grandfather? The knight of the Balthasar castle, Buryl. And it was not Raleigh. Why was Dugan's opinion important to her? His grandfather a hero. Would he approve? Was Buryl the knight she was looking for or a knight just like him? What had Iola thought of Buryl's antics, or was she also a part of them?

Regardless of the relationship Dugan had built up in his mind with his grandfather, he was still his grandfather and had his place in the family history. There could be not missing link.

After all Raleigh hadn't been such a saint himself. He had taken Silvia from another man. A promised and arranged relationship. Fought for her and won. Why should he judge Buryl?

Buryl had enjoyed all of life, joy, sorrow, laughter, secrecy, fear, tenderness, yes, the gamut of all human emotions. And was not afraid to enjoy them. He was a true knight. Not one to over look and push away. Hold on tight Buryl.

Calista could see Buryl in all these situations. See the smile of defiance on his lips. She wanted the treasures of Balthasar more and more with each though. What would she do if Buryl was not among the paintings? She desired to see an image of Buryl. Look into his face and see the meanness portrayed there. If Raleigh wouldn't lead her to the treasures, perhaps Buryl would.

Was the thought of all these ghosts floating about making Calista a paranoid lunatic? Was fantasy being confused with reality? With every creak and groan she turned to see if one of the Balthasar ghosts were watching and waiting.

Dugan had come over late after Calista he built a fire and was dreaming of how she would began her inscribing of Buryl. He just started talking about Buryl.

"When Buryl met Iola it was like sitting back and watching a movie. In what ways Buryl didn't think to rebel Iola did."

How would Dugan know all this? He wasn't there. How could this information be carried out to today's explanation? Did this family discuss itself even the evil? Wouldn't families keep things like this secret? After all the Balthasars seemed to enjoy secrecy.

"Iola came to Balthasar as a drama student. The static draw to Buryl came with the first sight of each other. The drama began in class and out.

Buryl would scheme ways to draw Iola from the classroom. Iola's desire was to be a great actress so many times she wouldn't cater to his whims.

When this happened Buryl would become eccentric and unpredictable. He even joined the drama class to be near her. She became his greatest folly in Raleigh's sight."

Calista was sure Dugan must be making all this story up from his own imagination. Is this the drama he had played out in his own mind? Was he pleased to have all this wickedness in his ancestry? Was he also wicked? Is this how he knew the sly underhanded immorality worked for their own benefit?

"The greatest mistake Raleigh made was to expel Iola from the school. Buryl and Iola wouldn't be separated. They didn't see themselves in a strange way. The whole world was crazy, everyone in it was crazy and they were the only normal ones.

Raleigh made every possible attempt to be rid of Iola. Only to drive her more into the arms of Buryl. Raleigh's last attempt brought Buryl and Iola to a marriage contract. With them walking in one evening and at dinner time, tossing their marriage decree in Raleigh and Silvia's face. They marched out of the room and into Buryl's living quarters in the castle."

How would Dugan know such intricate details of this evening? How had this history been told and by whom?

"Buryl and Iola tried every means possible to bring an acceptance of Iola into the family. They went out of their way and routine many times to do for Raleigh and Silvia. Nothing worked.

Iola continued her schooling in the drama class and Buryl also joined the class with much more fervent desire. They carried their frolics from the social life into the drama class and great plays were created. They performed in Belsar's best theaters along with the fall festivities on Balthasar grounds. They were the first to be discussed when performances were planed. Their conflict brought them success. Raleigh and Silvia would never attend these festivities."

Were these performances and festivities recorded somewhere in Belsar's archives? Calista couldn't help but think they were and somewhere in the archives she would be able to find and read these dynamic performances.

"If Raleigh and Silvia hadn't continually protested they would have become great stars. And brought great fame to the Balthasar name."

So Dugan did think highly of his grandfather. He had forgiven his recklessness. He would probably approve if Calista made Buryl a hero and of course now she would have to feature Iola also.

"Raleigh had worked so hard to get his school to be recognized and he was afraid that Buryl's rash decisions would bring rebuke to the school and students would break away. He didn't consider strutting around on a stage . . . work.

He intensely fought drama yet he allowed it to be taught in his school, only because it was recognized as one of the fine arts.

Raleigh and Silvia were continually being pressed to submit and accept Buryl and Iola's fame. The claw of persistence worked only once." Dugan paused for a time, fixed the fire and waited.

"They were present at Buryl and Iola's last performance. The play was in one of Belsar's finest theaters. The audience gave standing ovation and they were asked to do the last scene time and time again. Raleigh must surely have felt some pride."

In his eyes Calista could see the feeling of pride in Dugan. The fire of following your own dream and making it come true. Is that why he had so readily accepted her? She was following her dream, just as Buryl had from his childhood. Did Dugan know her dreams had prepared her for this work ahead?

"Buryl and Iola celebrated late into the evening. It was a stormy night and Buryl was killed in an accident on the way home, Iola survived.

Raleigh and Silvia surely must have regretted they had only seen one of their performances.

Iola was carrying a child at that time . . . my father. Seems like destiny was with the Balthasars to preserve a male child to carry on the Balthasar name. Had Iola died in the wreck it would have been the end of the lineage."

Dugan was the one to carry on now. Calista was glad she had the castle but felt a pang of sorrow that Dugan hadn't made it in time to purchase and keep the castle in the Balthasar name.

"To show they still protested the couples copulative marriage they wouldn't allow Iola to be buried in the family cemetery buy Buryl.

So she was buried on the knoll where you found the marker. I'm glad you found it."

"I'm so glad I found it also. We will have to clean it up and make it a special place."

"Legend has it that many times she has been seen standing on the knoll watching the castle for Buryl, her lover. They also say that times the lights come on in Buryl's rooms and signals his love to her as she waits.."

In Calista's dreams she had seen the ghost, the lights and the storm. What was the meaning of the storm? Was it the storm of Buryl and Iola's fight to be accepted? Was it a storm of wills, a dragon, a monster between herself and Dugan? Now her answer was clear all but the storm. Legends sometimes had some true meaning. She herself had stood on the knoll and watched the lights of the castle. Saw the ghostly figure march back and forth across the shadows. If the Balthasar history wasn't hers to do why had she been train in dreams from from infancy? Why had she dreamed even before she came here?

Why she felt so at home so connected with everything here? Were the spirits working? Calista needed answers to many questions.

"Iola gave up acting, stopped her classes, she had lost her leading man. No other could take Buryl's place. The drama class never produced another set of stars as Buryl and Iola.

"She left the Balthasar place and Raleigh and Silvia died thinking the lineage had come to an end with them. She used it as her punishment to them. Let them think no one would take the castle and go on with the dreams and the school. If they would have just accepted Iola she would have stayed. Carried on with the school and let Rawlins grow up on the grounds. But she felt that Raleigh and Silvia must suffer the heartbreak of never knowing. Rawlins was my father."

Calista was trying to understand Iola's reasoning. With this aimless corrupt act of being vile the Balthasar legacy had been lost. What a price to pay. Did getting revenge really bring her the pleasure she wanted?

"Ceara and I have sit at grandmother's feet and listened to her tales of life here at Balthasar. The passions of her love for Buryl, she carried to her death. The prison that held her most was the grieving for her lover and companion, Buryl. Their love was not play acting, not a rash passionate whim. If Raleigh and Silvia had only seen that their love was as strong and meant to be, just like their own.

The only sorrow Iola felt was that the legacy had been lost to Rawlins. She tried to make the loss up to him in many ways. He had lost the chance to grow up here and know his ancestry. But by the time he could have taken over, the castle was in ruins."

"Did he ever come here to see what his legacy would have been?"

"Yes, brought Iola here to be buried, saw the ruins, saw the work it would take and didn't think it worth the time."

"But it is worth it."

"You and I think it is. My father had established a good comfortable life and he didn't want to give it up. Other things happened while he was here. He became wild and was at first, a wild rogue. She had loved Buryl and she would love his son to the end, I know she would have, even his wildness."

"Where is your family now?"

"There is only Ceara and I left. We will get into it at a later date."

I was in the castle today and I see you and your workers have the classrooms almost to completion."

"The work has been hard but rewarding. Walter has been so much help. I was thinking just today that it is time to look for teachers and students."

"I have the tower ready for class. I have talked to some students that may be interested in coming here for their classes. Do you mind if I go ahead and start my classes?"

"Not at all. I want to do some writing for myself before I start teaching."

Calista didn't want to tell him at this time she was interested in bringing the Balthasar history up to date.

"Love seems to bloom here at the school. Lark and Aaron were expelled for finding a fancy for each other, and there have been others. You may want to consider what steps you want to take when this happens now."

"There won't be any steps taken. After listening and seeing the mistakes Raleigh made I think it is best to leave love emotions alone. Aaron and Lark, Buryl and Iola were mistakes taken. Nothing will be done."

"None?"

"None." Calista was so firm the conversation wasn't carried farther.

"Sounds reasonable."

"I've been making plans for the school. Let me tell you what I've planned and see what you think. Since you will be one of the teachers and will be affected by it. I think it can come to pass much faster this way."

Dugan sat and let her explain the financial plans for the school. Letting the teachers take their salaries for the students, giving a small percentage to her. Each teacher would be self-employed and responsible for their own bookkeeping.

He left the hearth where he had been sitting with his back to the fire. He came over to the chair facing her and took her hands in his and wouldn't let go.

"That is just the way Raleigh took care of business. He must be working with your thoughts. It worked perfect for him. He put the percentage the teachers gave him back into supplies and maintenance, taking only a small part to pay the servants and run the household."

"I think it would still work today."

"And so do I."

The excitement of the moment left them both speechless and deep into their own thoughts.

His hands were so warm as he held on to Calista She couldn't bring herself to pull away. The school would take care of itself.

"I think I should start to advertise for teachers."

"Ceara teaches music, but I don't think she would be willing to leave the city. She is a good teacher. She is also my agent when it comes to selling my art. I would miss her doing this for me."

"You could be together here. She wouldn't have to take no so many students that she could take care of your business. She could work out her own schedule What ever she wanted."

Dugan just stared into her eyes. That would please him and she understood how he would want her with him. The only part of his family that was left. He dropped her hands and paced the floor in front of the fireplace.

"It would work for her. She could bring the students she already has. It would work for her." He repeated. "If she could only be persuaded."

Calista left the castle early the next morning. She was going into Belsar to put an add in the paper for the school. She was ready to begin.

She stopped by Sugar Grove Inn to see how Lark and Aaron were doing and to see if anymore of her mail had come there. None had so she visited for awhile.

"How is Walter doing?" Lark seemed so concerned for his welfare.

"He seems to be happy to help around the castle. He knows what should be done next and goes about it like it is life or death to get it finished. Since I told him he was not leaving when the students started to come to the school."

"That would concern him, I'm sure. He doesn't stay around here when we have guests. He hasn't been to visit us since you came."

"Dugan is going to ask Ceara to move her students to the school and teach music. But he thinks she likes it in the city and will be hard to convince."

"She is a good teacher. Some of her students have given concerts here in Belsar. Sometimes she comes with them and sits in the audience."

"It would be good for her and Dugan to be together at the castle. I have told him she could set up her own schedule and still have some freedom. Dugan has told me what stars Buryl and Iola were."

"There is a lot of history to the school when it was in the beginning, it could be again. It was very successful."

"I have come today to put an advertisement in the paper for the school. Dugan thinks we have the castle near enough to completion to get started. He has the tower ready and wants to start with his art students now."

Lark seemed relieved to hear that Dugan was comfortable with the situation at the castle. Lark chatted on and on about what the school was like. She smiled and told Calista about her and Aaron falling in love and had to leave the school.

"We are so happy to be settled here in out little nest and have guests come and go. We haven't missed the school at all. Or the training we were getting."

Calista left and went to the post to see if she had any mail from Donel Ludwig. She was interested in her stock. Had it been sold ? She wanted to burn all her bridges with Wingate and Kemp Maston.

She had a letter from Donel and one from Kemp. The one from Kemp seemed to burn her fingers as she folded it and put it in her pocket. She started to throw it in the trash without even reading it, but decided against it.

Donel had sold the stock and she just stood in awe at the amount on the check. Yes, Kemp had purchased her stock and now had control of the company, just as she knew he would. What more would he have to say to her?

She took the letter from her pocket and walked to her truck. She was not so sure she could take anymore surprises standing up.

'I will be there to bring you back to Wingate. Calista that pile of rocks are not for you. He had written.

"No, no." She said aloud. I don't want to see you ever again.

Would he never give up and leave her alone. She became very irritated. She rushed back into the post and angrily scribbled him a post card not to waste his time. Don't come! She was happy here and wouldn't leave. Don't waste your time she wrote again.

The check would give her the funds to finish the castle and school the way she had planned.

She made her way to the bank and then on to the hardware store to inquire of some contractors to do the rest of the work. Her dream was going to be a reality soon just as Dugan had said. The air she was walking on was much lighter with every step. Reality, reality she kept saying to herself. Then her mother's words took over her thoughts. *"Knights are no more, Calista. Your dreams will take you on a path you don't want to travel."*

Had she been lost in the work at the castle that she had not heard those words for so long? No, mom-ree my dreams are going to be real, and she argued with her mother's words.

Chapter Eleven

alista was wallowing in her dreams when she was awaken by pounding. The noise was drowning her silent room. The fitful dreams left her muddled and disoriented for a time. She wanted the silence of the morning to wash away her dreams but the noise was intruding with her minds plans.

The noise was coming from the castle! She rushed to get dressed. Why would Walter be hammering so much there wasn't that much more to do until the contractors arrived with the supplies? They should be here sometime today but it was early. Surely they were not that studious.

She rushed to the door only to find to her amazement that Walter was directing the contractors. She watched on as he pointed here and there. He was doing just what she would be doing if she had been giving the instructions. Had Walter watched as she worked and knew what she wanted?

Maybe his mind wasn't lacking like she had preceded in the beginning. She didn't believe anyone to be an idiot.

And Walter had proven her right. He had pitched in with the work on the tower and had helped her with the castle. Dugan trusted him enough to give him jobs to do and go off and leave him to do them, so had she.

"What's going on?"

"So there you are? They were ready to start and I couldn't find you in the castle."

"I was trying to sleep. You seem to be doing just fine."

Walter picked up a piece of wood and handed it to the man.

"This young man seems to know what you want done so we just went ahead with the work."

"That's just fine," she gave her approval.

She stepped back and let Walter go on with the instructions. He was handling what was needed. Had Walter found his niche? He was making a good helper and impressing her with every action. Walter belonged here. He should have been a Balthasar instead of Dugan. Was Dugan not helping because he was afraid to interfere? Would Walter make a good living knight? Are knights always intelligent, and schooled? The story of Walter would make a good manuscript. Did she no longer have to look at the ghost of Buryl to find a knight? Walter belonged, knighthood suited him fine. She watched for awhile and then went back to the bailey castle.

Calista wondered around from room to room. She had enough intelligence to know she would be in the way of the workers in the main castle. This would be a good chance for her to go to Belsar and try to find history of Buryl and Iola. Her mind had the itch to began the manuscript to bring the history of the Balthasar family up to date. She had already written down all the tales Dugan had spun in the fire lit evenings. Her trust was in Walter to keep the workers on track.

She didn't even go to Sugar Grove Inn to visit Lark and Aaron. She went straight to the library.

"I'm looking for information on performances that were performed here when Buryl and Iola were actors in the drama class at Balthasar."

The librarian's eyes lit with a brightness, Calista knew she had found what she wanted.

"And what performances they were. You are in luck. We have film on file, not to rent or loan, but when you have the time we also have a viewing place where you can go and watch them, until you tire."

"I have time today."

"Then come with me. It will be hard for you to decide which film you want to watch. They are all so excellent. One is background and content of the castle where Buryl grew up. It is called, 'Can True Love Really Exist' and it is the best. It is one of my favorite documents and one I have watched over and over."

"That is the one I will watch today. I live at the castle."

"Oh, really. I thought one of the heirs had come back to claim the castle."

"That would be Dugan Balthasar. I purchased the property only days before his arrival."

"A man that leaves you wondering about the fire in his eyes."

Calista didn't feel like a response was necessary and remained silent as she followed the attendant to the viewing room. Others had also seen the fire in Dugan's eyes. She stopped only while the attendant pulled a worn and ragged film case from the shelf.

"You can see by the wear and tare of the case this film has been watched much."

"Do you keep records of who views the films?

"Oh, yes. And you will see that also. You too must sign and date the records."

The attendant opened the case and took papers from the case and spread them on the table. The smell of books and leather didn't distract Calista one bit. She hardly paid any attention at all to the smell and sounds around her. She had even stopped listening to the attendant. She was ready to take all the information from the film that she could gleen on the history of the Balthasars.

"You will see that I have watched it many times." She pointed to her name on the list, Yvonne Hart.

"I'm a relative of Walter Hart that has lived on the property grounds for years. I haven't kept in touch with him for awhile. Is he still there? He was a bastard child of one of my mothers aunts."

Calista wasn't listening to her chatter about Walter. Her babble had become only echoes in Calista's ears. But she did answer her question.

"Yes he is still there."

She was lost in the list before her. Lark and Aaron had seen the film. The other names meant nothing to her. Until she saw the last one, Dugan Balthasar. His name was there twice along with different dates. He had come and watched the film at two different times. Was he that interested in his grandfather, or was he just curious like herself? Had he watched the other films also.

Calista signed her name and date, settled in the chair before the screen and waited.

"When you have had enough just press this button. It will ring me."

Enough, how could she ever get enough of what had become so dear to her? Enough! No she would never get enough of the Baltharas. Some how the feeling of connection again became apart of her. She was in the Balthasar life to the very end. This was her new life. Wingate and her past was history. The only thing that haunted her was her mother's words. *"Calista, knights are no more."* That would always be a memory from her past.

The film began to roll and was carried away from reality and into the fantasy of drama. Her heart began to pound as the castle grounds spread before her on the screen. Who had painted this background with such accuracy? Buryl . . . Raleigh . . . the art class? The castle lay before her as she had visioned it would look when the restoration was complete.

The first sceen was of the drama class. Even with all the students in the room, a long haired student stood out immediately, one knew the story was going to be about her. Iola, that was Iola!

Now the faces of the Balthasars were becoming a reality. The tenderness and attraction was there as her long curls lay across her shoulder. There was a smile just under the surface of her face as if she was waiting for some fantasy to happen. Calista could see how Buryl could not resist. When would Buryl walk out on the stage so she could satisfy her desire to read his face and know if his recklessness could be seen?

The teacher went on and on in descriptions of drama, emotions and adding her own feelings and body language to the written words of the script. There would be many elements that would make up drama. How a play or movie would become teamwork along with the lighting, sounds, costumes and camera motions. The director could only make and demand the actions but the true emotions came from the actors themselves. Put yourself in an emotional position to stand out even though there are many actors in the script. Become good . . . bring into being what the true feelings of the author was. The script is the core of the performance but your actions puts the core to light. Always remember the character you are portraying is a human being even though they are made up. The writer of the script wanted the audience to believe they are a real person. Your character will become what your audience sees them act and do. An act is when the scene is over and no explanation is required.

Will your character be brave, fearful, resourceful, greedy, clever, violent, jealous a thief a liar or a hypocrite?

You won't be on the screen long before the audience will know and they will either love you or hate you. Every emotion you show, the audience has felt sometime in their life. They won't be seeing you they will be seeing themselves and reliving their own experiences.

Calista was caught up in these explanations thinking that is the same with writing a manuscript. One feels the characters emotions as the words fill the page. Stories, essays, plays and music are all the same, with the desire to stir the emotions of the audience or the reader.

She noticed a movement in the doorway behind the teacher and noticed the only student raising her head to look was Iola.

The esoteric smile that lay hidden spread across Iola's face and only the shadow of movement understood. Buryl stepped into view and the room grew much smaller with his presence and one could sense that it was unbearable for Iola to sit still.

Just as the teacher said turn to page 280 and let's read . . . Buryls flamboyant spirit drifted into the room following in his wake as it was separated form him body. If he had been riding a white stallion the electricity of the room couldn't have been more charged.

Calista caught her breath in utter surprise because Buryl was almost a mirror image of Dugan. The Balthasar fire was in his ocean blue eyes. Buryl extended his toward Iola, she dropped her book, took his hand and as their auras met and blended into a spiritual vibration all else in the room faded into the background. Buryl quoted the lines of love from the script as if he had written them himself. Iola responded with the same vibrant spirit.

The inexplicable tension went on from line to line, scene to scene as Buryl and Iola waltz around the stage hand in hand quoting feelings of love.

Calista's enlightenment came slowly. They were not quoting the text, they were making the text. This was true love and true drama.

Had the teacher planned this or was she using the miraculous magnetic pull between these two lovers as true acting which she would explain away after the charade was over? This is the kind of drama she wanted taught in her school, now to find such a teacher.

This was a biography of what had happened between Buryl and Iola. She could see why Raleigh and Silvia had no chance to separate such lovers. The Balthasar history, Dugan had recounted in the quiet evenings in the bailey castle before the firelight, Calista was believing more and more the stories Dugan had narrated to her were not fictious.

And she also was awakened to the fact that Dugan was truly Dugan Balthasar and Buryl was his grandfather.

There would be great stars again, great drama at the Balthasar school. The school would rise again and be a success. All the arts would be the best.

When the film was over she didn't want to leave. She wanted to see more. See them all and one day she would. Time and work would not let her stay longer.

Chapter Twelve

C alista went back to the castle wanting to see the contractors gone. She wanted to look the job over and see if it was being done to please her. It would be better to stop them early.

When she came into view she saw Walter standing with a notebook giving directions to the contractors. They were in front of the building doing something. What were they building? She had not given orders for anything to be built in the front yard. Then she saw someone else, Kemp! What was he doing here again? She had written him not to waste his time coming back. She was not in a mood to face him now, or was she?

She stopped her truck and jumped out to demand what they were building. Her eyes fell on the sign they were working on. It was dazzling.

She read the words, 'Balthasar School of Fine Arts-- Calista Iven, Director' The sign was what she wanted and had planed and drew in her notebook, wood with the words burnt into the wood, with vines bordering the left side and top, with stone posts. When had the stones been gathered?

"Are you pleased?" Walter was looking for approval as he stood holding her notebook. She just stood there surprised.

"Walter how did you know?"

He held out the notebook with the drawings she had made.

"See it's all right here. I have been working on it for some time. I hid the supplies away. I wanted to surprise you. Since you have been so good to me. Lark and Aaron has been good to me too."

Walter began to ramble with words, muttering to himself. He turned away and stared at the workers. The Workers just stood listening.

"How did you find my notebook?"

The tone of her voice must have frightened him for he looked at her as if he was afraid. He had transgressed. Calista could almost read his emotions and she was sorry she had spoken so roughly to him.

"No, no Walter. It's alright. It is just the way I had perceived."

"I used your drawings. See." He pointed to her notebook.

Calista patted his shoulder to show him it was just what she wanted.

"There is nothing to be afraid of."

"I wanted to surprise you." He repeated.

"You did surprise me . . . and what a surprise."

"Then you . . ."

"I didn't think we would get this far today."

"You have company. That man is here again." He turned and pointed at Kemp. His disgust was apparent.

In her excitement she had forgotten about Kemp.

"Why are you here? Did you not get my note. I told you not to come."

"I came to take you back to Wingate."

Walter rushed to her side and put his arm around her shoulder.

"She's not going anywhere."

"That's right . . . I'm not."

"Calista you have done miracles with the restoration, but this is not the place for you. Leave it to others. You should be in Wingate and a part of the company, there is no destination we can't reach." He stood staring into her face as if nothing else mattered. "With your knowledge and my understanding of the company we can take it to the top."

"Kemp it isn't a frontier company," she was irritated. "It is already established and only needs someone with direction to take it where you want it to go." She knew since he had the controlling interest he would take it where he wanted with or without her. No, without her. That was going to be the way it was.

"I want you back in Wingate."

"Calista belongs to us." Walter tightened his arm around her shoulder and stood his ground.

"Us? Kemp's tone and stare gave the impression, he wanted Walter to stay out of this. "Us," he repeated, "and pray tell who is US?" he shook his head at Walter.

No, Calista thought, she would not let Kemp intimidate Walter. He had been hurt enough in the past, and she had promised him he would not be hurt again by anyone. Not the townspeople, teachers, or the students. She had resigned herself as his protector, and protect him she would. She took a determined stance. She fixed her look on Kemp and didn't flinch until he looked away and relaxed his shoulders.

"Did you not get my card telling you not to waste your time coming back here?"

"I did. You need to be pressured . Your place is in Wingate."

"My place is here."

"I don't want loneliness for you Calista."

"Lonely, I'm not lonely."

"When all this fails and everyone is gone, that is what I'm thinking of. Loneliness will come and it will be to late."

"Loneliness comes from within. I'm happy, content and secure inside. I won't harbor loneliness."

"There won't be anything you can do about it. Take care of it now."

"I have been in town doing business for the school, and I'm in no mood to be burdened with more. If that is all, I have work to do." She took Walter's hand and gave it a pat. "I'm not going anywhere."

"Me and Dugan wouldn't let you anyway." He didn't try to hide his contemptuous smile.

Calista turned and watched as Walters shoulders rose and fell, as if to say "Now what?" He turned to Kemp and stood there looking at him for a long time without saying a word. Then he stepped back put his hands on his hips and said

"I think she's through with you."

Calista stood back and watched form the castle window. Walter walked back to the workers. Kemp watched Walter and the workers for sometime. It was apparent they were unmindful of Kemp as they worked.

She smiled to herself, content that Walter had grown enough to handle anything Kemp dished out. Was she his protector or he hers? His rugged living had made him strong and he would make a good security guard for the school. He had come a long way since the first day she arrived and was doing a great job with the work. He seemed to know what she wanted and went about doing it. She hadn't taken her notebook from him thinking he may be more secure with her approval of the work he was doing. Was the Balthasar ghosts working with Walter also?

She turned to her computer and begin to create application forms for the school. Yes, she was pleased with Walter and didn't look up when she heard Kemp's car drive away.

Her office was set up at the foot of the stairs and the beginning of the classrooms, overlooking the front yard. She could watch the teachers and students arrive each morning and greet them. She raised her head and looked out at the sign, surprised she noticed the sign could be read from both sides. She had over looked it when she was putting up with Kemp. She breathed a sigh, almost sure she would never have to confront him again. He was gone from her life and she was relieved.

Calista rested her head on her palms wondering if teachers would be interested in teaching in a private school where they would be responsible for their own income.

It had worked for Raleigh. Dugan had thought that it would still work, and so did she, yet she was concerned. Had her mother been right? Would she have spent all this time and effort for a downfall? If there was a downfall she would still be content for the attempt of trying.

"Calista! Are you all right?"

"Walter?"

"Are you asleep?"

"No I was just lost in thought."

"You have another visitor. Will this happen often?" He looked irritated at the interruption.

"Another man is here to see you. I made him wait outside. Do you want to see him? He said he was a teacher."

"Oh, yes, bring him in."

"I didn't wait outside." A skinny petite man jumped into the room pushing Walter aside. He caught Calista by the hand, bowed low and pulled Calista from her chair and danced around the room. He hadn't even waited for introductions.

"I'm here in answer to your ad for a teacher of drama. Your problems are over."

He turned her lose and danced around the room again quoting poetry. Walter just stood shaking his head

"Do you want this?"

"It's all right Walter. I can take care of this."

"Then I'll go back to work."

Calista watched while the teacher all but bounced off the walls. She wanted drama not play acting, serious drama, like the teacher she she had seen in the film of Buryl and Iola. This would just be like a circus act, nothing like the drama the school had before. All that she had seen and heard of the school during Raleigh's time was nothing like this. She picked up an application and handed it to him while he was still in motion.

"Well?"

"Well . . . we're still working on classrooms and they are not quiet ready to start with students. Where are you teaching now? Fill out this application, return it with a resume and reference letters."

"That's it? I have four students ready to come with me to the school. We have heard a lot about the school that was here before and the theater that's here. Plenty of room to work and play."

Play Calista thought. Play is not what I want. I want drama.

"Have you seen any of the films, in the library of the drama class that was here before?"

"No, what does that have to do with today's drama?" He seemed uninterested in any of the works of the old school.

"I suggest you go view some of them and learn from them. That kind of drama is what I want for this school."

"That won't help my teaching."

She didn't think anything would help his teaching. Was this what audiences wanted today? "Turn in what I ask." She was strong with her words.

This is not what I want she kept telling herself. Is this what drama is about today she ask herself again, fun and games? Not in my school. She wanted classic drama, serious drama and serious students. Student wanting to learn and be great actors. Drama not comedy! She wasn't against a good laugh once in a awhile, not what she wanted in this school. She had been to the library and had experienced good drama. She took him by the arm and escorted him out of the room toward the door.

Walter was still standing by the door with an astounding gaze.

"What was that about?" He ask when the teacher left.

"Was that drama?"

"Not in my book it wasn't. He wants to be the teacher of the drama class."

"Is he going to be one of the teachers?"

"No he isn't."

Walter seemed to relax. Threw his hands in the air and walked away mumbling to himself.

Hiring teachers wasn't going to be as easy as she thought. Had times changed so much? How long was it going to take to fill the positions for the classes? Good teachers. Walter would be a big help in her choosing. He seemed to know her thoughts, and seemed to understand people. Yes, he was going to be a big asset to the school. Had his trouble with the townspeople taught him well? Drama not comedy she said to herself again and went back to making applications knowing from this experience she was going to need more. This wasn't going to be easy.

How would she break the news to the applicants when they were not want she wanted? She had never been in the position to hire and fire, yet she wanted the best teacher available. She was going to be very selective when she started to hire.

When would Cerea come? Dugan said she was interested. She stopped typing and walked to the music room. It had been cleaned up and was ready. It was a large room overlooking the tower. A movement drew her to the window. Dugan was going to his car with a large picture wrapped in paper. Had he had time to paint a picture already, or had he found the treasures and was taking them from their hiding place? She had the urge to run and ask him, but she held herself back. If Dugan was going to be a teacher and she was going to work with him, she would have to trust him.

Was Dugan really a Balthasar? Doubt slipped in again. Come on Calista you have been to the library and saw Buryl in action and he is the mirror image of Dugan. Yes Dugan is a Balthasar. Walter trusted him and so would she. The Balthasar stories had been told with a plausible understanding, and he had a sister with the same name as her research had revealed. Lark and Aaron recognized them as Balthasars. They had kept in touch with them through the years.

I must trust and not be suspicious of everyone here. Had all this work and the interview with the first teacher made her paranoid of everyone?

"*Calista, Calista knights are no more. Your dreams will take you on a path you will not want to travel.*" Her mother's words had haunted her for so long.

Was she tired both mentally and physically from all this rush to get the school ready? When would she stop having so many questions and doubts?

Was Dugan steeling the paintings? Had he been told where they were? Is that why he insisted on having the tower?

She leaned against the wall with an exasperated mind, thoughts and doubts running wild. Kemp, Dugan, Cerea, teachers, students Balthasar place, Walter and the Balthasar ghosts, would all these drive her insane?

These thought ran scrambled through her mind all evening. Was she on a path she didn't want to go as her mother had predicted? No, she was just tired . . . tired. The first interview with a teacher and she was tired. Were all these going to be to much for her alone? All she had wanted to do was write and she was neglecting it. Balthasar history, stories, ghosts and writing all seemed to close in on her at once. What was real, what was truth and what was fiction? Calista thought she was strong enough to handle anything but these scrambled thought running through her mind was giving her doubts and fears of her own strength. Have I taken on more than I can handle? Who could she go to for advice, Kemp? She could give all this up and go back to Wingate and live peacefully with Kemp.

Calista ran to the window at the sound of an approaching car. Kemp was back and walking toward the castle door.

"What are you doing back here?" Her irritation and nerves had reached their limit.

"I didn't leave Balsar. I am not giving up until you go back to Wingate. I came to force you to go."

"I'm not going anywhere. How many times do you have to be told?"

"And where is that idiot that thinks he is your bodyguard?" He didn't even loose a breath as he kept looking over his shoulder for Walter to appear.

Calista's reaction was to slap Kemp as hard as she could but she drew back.

"Don't you ever say that word in my presence again. And never those words on this property."

"Idiot . . . idiot." Kemp was loosing control.

"Get out." She started toward him and he kept backing up with every step she took. "Get out of here now."

The anger in her face and voice backed him to the door.

"Get out . . . get out."

"What's going on here?" Dugan had both hands on Kemp's shoulders. Kemp flinched.

"Nothing!" Kemp said without turning around. He knew this was not the idiot's voice.

"Oh yes something is, Calista?" Dugan was waiting for her answer.

"Nothing, Kemp was just leaving and he won't be back again." The anger was still on Calista's face and in her voice. She wanted to tell Dugan she could handle this but she felt safe in his presence.

"Calista?" Softness had taken over Dugan's voice.

"Is there nothing really wrong? Kemp was just leaving?"

Dugan spun him around and gave him a forceful shove toward the door. Kemp started to turn but changed his mind in mid-turn. He walked to his car muttering.

"Idiot . . . idiot. All are idiots."

Calista started after him but Dugan caught her in his arms and held her close.

"Alright what is going on? You are shaking."

"Where is Walter?"

"Down on the rocks. Now what's going on, and what does Walter have to do with this?"

"He called Walter and idiot. I promised Walter I wouldn't let anyone ever call him that again."

"No harm done. He didn't hear."

"But if he had been near he would have heard."

"Again, no harm done. Sit down and calm yourself." He let go of her and took after Kemp.

Calista watched as Dugan caught Kemp at his car. Dugan opened the door but blocked the entrance. Calista wished she could hear what Dugan was saying, but from his body language, she almost knew. Dugan stepped aside and again gave Kemp a shove into the car. Dugan slammed the door and motioned Kemp to start the car and be gone. Kemp stared. Dugan was reaching for the door latch but Kemp started the car and spun out. Dugan watched until he was out of sight before turning back to the school.

Calista walked to her chair and fell into it before her legs gave away.

"Who is this guy" He has been here twice before to cause trouble."

"He is a high school classmate that thinks he can get anything he wants."

"I don't think he will be coming back."

"I hope not."

"He won't. How much of our conversation did you hear?"

"None, I read your face."

"My face?"

"Yes, your face. You were fighting mad."

"Yes, I was. He called Walter an idiot. Walter is not an idiot."

"No he isn't. I promised him no one would ever call him that again."

"He whispered into her hair. "They won't ever again. At least not that guy I seen to that."

"They won't." She whispered back and feeling safe in Dugan's arms.

"What's going on?" Surprise was in Walters voice.

Calista jumped from Dugans touch.

"I thought I heard a car."

"You did hear a car. That fellow came to take Calista away again. The one you told me about."

Walter rushed to Calista and took her arm.

"You're not going anywhere."

"No I'm not. I think it is settled this time."

Dugan looked at Walter with a look of promise. "I told you the last time we wouldn't let her go anywhere so don't fret."

"He's not going to give up."

"This time he has I'm sure."

Dugan wanted to know about the last time he was there and how Walter handled it.

"So He thinks Walter is your bodyguard. Now he knows you have two bodyguards."

Walter began to tell him all about it and she stood and agreed. They continued to talk about the last time. Walter had told him about the last time but he wanted to hear it again. Because Walter had been worried enough to tell him about it.

"I'm not going anywhere."

"We know." The both said in unison. They all three began to laugh.

"I'm not going anywhere," She said again and hugged them both.

Chapter Thirteen

Calista had been to Belsar and visited with Lark and Aaron. She had talked to the them about the drama class and finding it hard to find a teacher that she was pleased with. Lark mentioned several names and then told her why didn't she talk to the librarian. She is interested in the films of Buryl and Iola. She watches them over and over. She may have some names she can suggest. She sees a lot of people and several times she talks them into watching the films. She has watched them many time herself.

"I have watched one of them. I'm sure it was the first one with Buryl and Iola. It had the drama class in it. I came today to watch another one. I want to see them all."

"Aaron and I go together and watch them. We have seen them all. They are real drama."

"That is what I want for the school. The teacher in that film was an excellent teacher. I liked her approach."

"She is still living but she is getting pretty old. She may know a few names she could give you. I'll write her telephone number down for you. Her name is Zenna Othman. It would be a pleasure to her if you visited. She don't have much company. I go over and usually take her one of my cakes. She's adorable.

"Will come back another time and go see her. I will call her first. I want to see another film today."

"I will tell her to expect your call and tell her why you are interested. It is time I go see her again."

Calista went straight to the library. She talked to Yvonne Hart. Mrs. Hart gave her a long list and Zenna Othmans name was on the list so was Aleah Kelvin. She was surprised Calista wanted to see another film. She took her back to the viewing room and ask what she wanted to see today.

"What is your next favorite?"

"They are all so good it would be hard to decide."

"Do you have the last film Buryl and Iola performed?"

"Yes we do."

"I would like to see it."

"It's a little long do you have the time?"

"I will make the time."

She took the film down and put it in the machine.

"Just ring me when you are finished."

Calista had notice Dugan had also seen this film. The film began to roll and Calista sat mesmerized for the three hours. How could Raleigh and Silvia not have gone to all the performances? But this was the only one they had seen. Were they disappointed that they had not been to all of them. They had miss so much by their stubborn unyielding attitude.

Calista went back to Balthasar and saw Walter wondering around. Dugan must be painting again and wouldn't let him watch.

"Walter come over here. We now have telephone lines. I will show you the rocks on the computer."

"Ok," he said joyously and ran to her.

She booted up the computer and typed in a few words and the rocks come up on the monitor.

Walter jumped back. "How did they get my rocks to take the pictures. I had them hid . . . hid well. Did Aaron find them and sell them to take the pictures?"

"No Walter Aaron wouldn't sell your rocks. These are not your rocks.

Other people collect rocks too. These are their rocks."

"But they look like my rocks. I have one like this one." And he pointed to some of the others. "I have some like these too. This is my favorite one."

Walter had pointed to an amethyst a light purple.

"Walter no wonder you like that one it's your birthstone."

"Birthstone? What is that?"

"Each month has a gem for its birthstone. That is my favorite one also. We were both were born in February and it is our birthstone."

Calista got up and went to a box on her table and took out a chain with an amethyst on it.

"See this was made from a rock just like yours. My mom and dad gave me this one for my sixteenth birthday."

"It's pretty. You never wear it. Pretty things should be worn. I would wear it."

"I want to keep it just like it is so I put it away. I remember my mom and dad each time I look at it."

"I don't have anything to remember my mom." He slumped over in sadness.

"You have your memories."

"Do you not have memories?"

"Yes and some very good ones. Let's look at some more rocks."

Calista scrolled from page to page. Walter became more and more excited. He pointed at several rocks and nodded his head. Calista thought each rock Walter pointed at he must have on like it.

"What are you two doing?" Dugan said as he walked into the room.

"Looking at rocks!" Walter said and motioned for Dugan to come over.

"Don't you have enough rocks to look at outside?

"Not like these rocks these are gems and I have some of them."

"Walter collects rocks."

"I want you two to come over to the tower. I have something to show you."

Clista closed the computer and her and Walter followed Dugan to the tower. He pulled a cover from a painting.

"You have painted me." Walter started to clap his hands. "Look Calista, Dugan has painted me."

"Yes he has and it is a good picture."

"I am sitting on my cliffs and looking at the sea. See how the mist is rolling over the water? How did you know that Walter sits there a lot and watches."

"I see you down there a lot and know what you are doing. When you get your own place you can hang the picture there. I will keep it for you until then."

Chapter Fourteen

Calista was restless. She prowled from one classroom to another. Some of the classes would start soon. Cerea would be here over the weekend to get her classroom ready for the music lessons which would began on Tuesday. Dugan planed to start his the same day.

She walked into the music room and looked at the piano that had been sent ahead. It would be nice to have some sound ring out and echo through the stone walls.

Calista walked over to the piano and raised the cover and hit the octave C chord. Yes it would be a pleasing entity. Music had not been her forte but she could sit and enjoy it for hours. Would Cerea play for them in the evenings? She hoped she would. Would she have recitals for her students? The room was big enough for the students and their parents.

She hit the chord again and closed the cover. She listened as the sound reverberated through the room and around the castle walls.

Where had Walter and Dugan gone today? They had been keeping secrets among themselves lately. What could they be up to? It seemed so strange not to have them around. Was Kemp correct in saying she would be lonely when all failed and everyone was gone. She didn't want to think of Kemp ever being correct about anything. As

Walters words rang in her mind, *"I think she is through with you."* She smiled to herself and thought yes, Walter is right I'm through with you forever.

She had not failed. The school would be a success.

She began to stray through the rest of the classrooms. The drama room . . . she had yet to find a drama teacher. Was she being to strict in her thinking of what drama should be? She walked upon the stage and stood in the center and let her mind run free. It would be the best.

"Calist knight are no more. You will be led down a path that you will not want to go." Her mothers words hadn't haunted her for some time now. There had to be an end to all these haunting doubts.

She walked off the stage and went to sit in the bleachers. Looking at the stage she could see Buryl and Iola.

She had been to the library and the librarian had given her a list of names, Lark had given her a list of names and Zenna Oatman had given her a list of names and there was one name that appeared on all the lists Aleah Kelvin. Was this her teacher? She had her number but she hadn't called. This is something she must do. She would ask her to come in for an interview and ask her if she was interested.

The shadows fell through the castle making Calistas emotions even more confound. The twilight was filling the room with emotions that Calista was not ready to harbor. She walked to the front door and opened it and looked out. The knoll seemed to draw her to it.

The was twilight but still light enough for her to walk up there and spend some time with the spirits of Iola and Buryl who had created the kind of drama the school deserved and what she wanted.

Calista stood on the knoll and closed her eyes and the mist and fog began to rise around her. Walter had told her the fog would come with great speed at times. She let the feeling of the school, the estate and the Balthasars take her emotions away. She drifted into the past listening to the spirits talk. They all jumbled together, from the tales Dugan had told, until she wanted to scream out please tell me what to do.

When she opened her eyes it seemed like she was in a mist looking through a dream. Just as her childhood dream had been. She gazed down at the castle. It was no longer in ruins.

The lights were on in her upstairs window. Her feet began to move and rested beside the marker of Iola. It seemed as the mist and fog were coming and rested on the grave for a few minutes an then took wings and drifted toward the castle window. Was Buryl waiting? Would they to be together again tonight?

Iola should be with Buryl. She must have a talk with Dugan and Ceara. Iola's body must be exhumed and placed in the family cemetery beside Buryl. Then and only then would the spirits rest. This discussion must be done soon.

Why should she discuss this with Dugan and Ceara she had bought the property and she had control of what was to happen. Out of respect for the Balthasar family she would discuss it with them but the final decision would be hers. Surely they would want them together, their grandfather and grandmother.

Tomorrow, yes she would talk to Dugan until his thoughts harmonized with her own and they would stand together with the terms that Iola and Buryl should be together. Would this be the storm of her dreams? She would always watch for that storm and would know when it appeared.

If Dugan and Ceara being the last of the Belthasars agreed that Iola had the honor to be a Balthasar from the beginning it would an honorable thing to do. Raleigh and Silvias anger and denial was in the past. She spoke aloud, "Iola, I will not let this rest until you are together."

Chapter Fifteen

C alista sat at her desk going over some applications that had been turned in. If Aleah Kelvin worked out she would have all her teachers except dance. The dance instructors all seemed to be qualified with good references. She had chosen Kieran Keelan for the first interview and he was to come sometime over the weekend. He was Irish and she knew the Irish were good dancers. She had always liked their native music and dance. If he didn't work out she had pulled two more applications out and placed them aside.

She had called Aleah Kelvin and she was interested and had a sound testimony of what drama should be. Calista ask her to go to the library and watch the film of the drama class from the former school before she came for the interview. She had said she would. Aleah was supposed to come today for the interview.

Calista kept her eyes on the window. They had agreed upon a ten o'clock appointment. It was getting close to that time and Calista wondered if she would be prompt and dependable.

This job of choosing teachers was not as easy as she thought it would be. How had Raleight selected his teachers for success? That was her main goal, success.

At fifteen until ten she saw a vehicle coming out the lane. She went down the steps and waited for her. When she heard the knock she opened the peep door and ask if she was Aleah Belvin and let her in. She took her to the downstairs office. They talked for some time and Calista said. "Come I will show you the drama room."

Aleah seemed to be excited about the room.

"I will let you look around at what you want to. I will wait here on the front bleacher."

"That will be nice," she said and started walking about the room. She walked upon the stage and looked back at the bleachers.

"It is a nice big room."

Then she looked at the holding rooms on each side of the stage, and came back down where Calista was. She walked to the top of the bleachers and sat down. She told Calista to go to the back of the stage and sing a song or quote some poetry.

Calista went to the back of the stage and sang a little song her mother had taught her, 'Jesus wants me for a sunbeam.' Then Aleah ask her to come to the front of the stage and sing in her normal voice.

"You were singing a little loud since you were in the back. That wasn't necessary. Now sing as if you were talking to someone standing beside you."

I'm not the one for the interview, you are, Calista thought. When she finished the song Aleah motioned her down.

"The accostics in this room are perfect. It is designed to control sound. Whoever built this room knew what they were doing. You could have whispered and I think I would have heard you."

Had Raleigh built this room or had he hired a professional Calista wondered?

Aleah took the job and said to give her a week and she would start the classes.

"I already have some students that want to come with me and they are going to inquire around and find some more. I already have some plays. I think we can be as good as the ones in the film."

"That is the kind of drama I want for this school."

"And we shall have it. I will see you again Monday a week and bring the students."

Calista went to her office and took out her log book and filled in the spaces for the drama class. She turned the pages in the book until she came to the dance page and stared at it a long time. One more and I will have all the teachers the school will need. She smiled to herself, leaned back in her chair and pretended she was listening to Irish music.

"What is the smile for?" Dugan said as he walked into the room.

"I just hired a teacher for the drama class. It was an interesting interview. I think she will be good. I had her go to the library and watch the film of Buryl and Iola before she came. And she thinks we can have just as good. We will have stars born again."

"But they won't be as good as Buryl and Iola. They were the best. I wish their lives hadn't been cut off so soon."

"So do I. That is a good film."

"So you have seen it? It was the first one to be recorded."

"I seen it and the last one they recorded. A lot was lost in that accident."

"It was the only one Raleigh and Silvia attended."

"Dugan I would like to discuss something with you. I have found Iola's grave. Have you ever thought of having her taken up and buried beside Buryl? She should be in the family cemetery."

"That is one of the things I had let pass through my mind when I was planning to purchase the property. Raleigh and Silvia are no longer in control. You now have control. Have you found the family cemetery?"

"No but I should think it wouldn't be hard to find."

"There may not be room for her beside Buryl. We must find the cemetery and see if there is room. Are you to busy this afternoon to go with me to find it?"

"That is a good idea. Yes I will go with you. I have just a few things to finish and I will be ready."

They met on the front lawn. Not knowing which way to start to look.

Calista wanted to go to the knoll. She hadn't thought to look from there for directions.

"Let's go to the knoll and look around and see if we can get any directions where to start."

Dugan was silent but nodded his head and started up the hill. As they walked to the knoll in silence Calista wondered why she hadn't seen the cemetery or the open air theater when she rode the property with the agent. Was this another one of the Balthasar mysteries.

"Have you seen Walter today?" Dugan ask.

"No I haven't. But look there he sits on the cliffs looking at the sea like the picture you painted. Lark said he lived here at the property for a long time. So you think he may know where the cemetery is?"

"It would be a good start to ask him. We could roam around and still not find it."

They walked to the cliffs and sat down by Walter and enjoyed the stillness for awhile. Then Calista tapped him on the shoulder and asked.

"Walter do you know where the Balthasar family cemetery is?"

"Yes it's not far. I'll take you there. There are lots of dead people there. I don't go there much. But I will take you."

They walked a short distance. There were lots of markers. Many names Dugan recognized. He read them aloud.

"Some of these were the servants, and here are the babies that were stillborn. Yet they wouldn't put Iola here."

"Look there is room for her. Now we can put her here."

Walter looked at her with a strange look.

"She is dead and already on the knoll. How can you put her here?"

Dugan and Calista explained to Walter how people can be exhumed and buried again. They took their time and repeated some of the information again and again. They were not sure he understood but he looked satisfied.

"Dugan look up there it is the theater. We have had a productive day."

They walked past the theater on their way back to the castle.

Chapter Sixteen

*I*t was Saturday morning the weekend was here. Kieran Keelan had called and ask if he could come for the interview. Calista went to the ballroom and was looking around. It had been restored and cleaned. It was a large room where many balls had been held. This room will be full again with music and dancing Clastia thought.

Mr. Keelan had also said he had several students that were interested in coming with him to the school. Calista wondered if it was curiosity.

"This is a very large room." Dugan said as he walked into the room.

"I just hope the accostics are as good in this room as they are in the drama room. Aleah said they were perfect."

"I would like to see all the classrooms if it wouldn't be an inconvenience. Ceara's classroom is the only one I have been in. It doesn't have to be today."

"It won't be an inconvenience. I will show them to you. Since you have seen this one the drama classroom is the only one left. When you get through looking at this one I will show you the other."

He took a few minutes to look around.

"Do you dance?" He ask.

"I only tried it once at my high school prom." Calista shivered inside. That dance had been with Kemp and neither of them were very good. She had never tried again. "It isn't a very good memory. My feet hurt for days from being trampled. Do you dance?"

"I never seemed to have the time to learn. Ceara and I tried it a few times at home with no teaching therefore it wasn't a very successful try so we gave it up."

"Would you like to see the drama classroom now? How about acting did you ever try your luck with it."

"Not in this lifetime, no. I left that talent to my grandfather and grandmother. I would rather observe."

They walked to the drama classroom. Calista knew it was going to be a touching moment for Dugan. He stood and stared at the stage. Was he seeing Buryl and Iola performing? What was he thinking? It sent cold chills down her spine when she thought of them meeting there and performing.

"Aleah said she believed you could even hear a whisper in this room it is built so well. I have stood here so silent trying to hear Buryl and Iola whispering to each other."

"Are you a mind reader? I was listening for the same thing."

"I miss sitting in the floor by my grandmother's chair and listening to her tales of their episodes."

"There presence is so heavy in this room as if they still occupy it. I hope the teacher will let me sit in on some of the skits. I would like to observe some of the students. The teacher had said they were good and didn't mind correction. Would stars be born again here in this very room?

They heard a loud "Hello" and went to the front to see if it was Kieran Keelan. Dugan had left the door open and he had come into the castle.

"I just came on in the door was open. I'm Kieran Keelan.

"I'm Calista Iven and this is Dugan Balthasar."

"Are you a Balthasar heir? I've heard so much about the time they were here."

"Yes I am. I will be going so you can go on with your interview." He said to Calista.

"I would like it very much if you would stay. I have brought music and you will be a help."

Dugan looked at Calista for her approval."

"Stay." She said. "Let's go to the ballroom."

The teacher was impressed with the size of the room.

"I can just see a ball being held here. I will start with a waltz first. It is the easiest to learn. Do either of you dance?"

They both shook their heads with a surprised look.

"You will start to learn today." His smile was contagious.

He started his music and took Calista by the hand and put her arm on his shoulder and gave instructions as he began to move. Soon they were moving about the room with ease. The music stopped and he started it again.

"Now you Mr Balthasar."

He placed Calista's arm on Dugan's shoulder and his hand on her waist. He walked beside them giving instructions. They were soon gliding about the room as the teacher stepped back and began to applaud.

"Now see how easy you learn. This is my form of teaching. I have some great ballroom dancers. Now Ms. Iven let's try the polka."

She looked at Dugan. "You didn't step on my toes one time."

He looked down at her feet. "And neither did you step on my toes. I just bet we have happy feet."

The teacher put on polka music and it was a little faster. Calista wondered if she would be able to keep up.

He took Calista's hands and moved her out on the floor and gave instructions.

"The polka will be a little more time consuming to learn."

They danced for awhile. He was changing the moves and let her keep up the dancing on her own for a while. Then he joined her again.

"That was a little harder but much more fun and much more tiring. It is a pretty dance."

"It can be a very inspiring dance."

"Now you Mr. Balthasar. It is a little harder but don't give up."

Dugan and Calista did more laughing than dancing at first. Soon they were at ease and doing fine. So the instructor said.

They discussed the school and what he would require. There would be chairs along the walls, and a table for the music.

"When do you plan to start classes?"

"Dugan has already started his classes. Every other class will be starting Monday of next week is that to soon for you?"

He agreed to be ready and bring his students and ask her if she would be joining or at least watching?

Chapter Seventeen

Today Iola was to be exhumed and placed by Buryl in the family cemetery. Dugan had given his class assignments and freed himself, and so had she. Ceara had to be in town for some of her students that didn't come to the school. She would not be able to witness the transfer but wanted to. Calista hadn't seen Walter all morning. He had not been on the cliffs. Was he aware of what would be happening today?

Calista and Dugan walked to the knoll and waited for the workers. When she looked around she saw Walter sitting on the ground at the edge of the woods. She motioned for him to come down. He shook his head yet he was watching.

She noticed how carefully the workers took the marker up and cleaned it off and placed it out of the way.

When the casket was exhumed and placed on the wagon Walter stood up. Calista thought he would come down but he had disappeared.

Dugan and Calista led the way to the family cemetery and showed the workers where Iola would be placed.

When the workers began to dig she looked and there sat Walter. She wondered what he was thinking and if he was scared. She hoped he wasn't. She whispered to Dugan and told him not to look but that Walter was watching.

He whispered back, "I hope this doesn't affect him. He is so sensitive."

She nodded approval and hoped Walter approved in what was happening.

When all was finished and the workers were gone Walter caught up with her and Dugan.

"Will the mist still come to the knoll now?"

"I don't know Walter but we will watch and see."

School was back to regular schedule. Calista went to the window every evening and every morning looking for the mist. None appeared. At last she thought Iola's spirit is free. Buryl and Iola were together again. She saw Walter on the cliffs each day watching. The mist had come to the water and cliffs but never back to the knoll.

School had been dismissed for the day and Ceara and Calista was standing in the hall talking when they heard notes being played on the piano.

They slipped to the music room and peeped in. There was Walter at the piano. His fingers went up and down the keyboard. Then he started to play. They could almost hear the hiss of the lightening and the roll of the thunder over the waters. It was easy for them to imagine. The storm went on for a long time.

"He has heard and seen the storms of the sea so much he has it memorized in his head." Calista said. "The storm was so real."

Ceara said with emotion, "He has made you and me see and hear the storm."

"Will he hurt the piano from playing so violent?"

"No and I wouldn't stop him if it did. Music is very relaxing even if it is so powerful and strong. He has a natural ability for sound. Not many people do."

Walter started to get up and they hurried away. Calista thought this was the storm of her dream. The dragon that lived inside of Walters head.

Calista raced up the steps. She didn't want to miss the knoll in the twilight. Would the mist come again? She stumbled and fell one of the steps tilted up. She slid back down and pulled it lose. I was hollow and full of spider webs when she peeped down. She stared for awhile. She could see a pencil streak of light. The light was coming from the drama classroom.

She walked down the steps and went into the classroom and started to feel around the wall where she thought the light was coming in under the steps. The wall was lose and she pushed and pushed on it until it began to slide.

When she got it open it was dark inside the space. She went back up the steps and removed the lose board and went back down to the classroom. There was a little more light and she could see things stored in the space.

She couldn't tell what any of it was. She was going to need more light. Had she found the treasures?

She went back up the steps to her room and searched and searched. She knew she had a flashlight somewhere. The last place she had used it was in the bailey castle but she had brought everything over to her apartment. Where could it be? Looking in her closet she saw her trunk and opened it. There it was. She hoped the batteries were still good. She tried it, they were! Hurrying back down the steps to the space under the steps she turned on the light.

Oh yes! She had found the treasures. There were the paintings, a table, chairs, vases and many other things. Why had she doubted Dugan? Then the light fell on a journal laying on the floor behind the table. Raleigh's journal! She put the light on the table and held the journal in front of it. Yes it was Raleigh's journal. She took the light and journal, closed the space and went to clean the journal to see if it had been damaged by mice or spiders.

It hadn't been damaged but had faded some. It could still be read.

"I will have to show this to Dugan." she said aloud and started toward the tower. Walter was ready to knock on the door.

"You are not supposed to open the door without peeping out."

"Walter would you please run over to the tower and ask Dugan if he has time to come over here?"

When Walter and Dugan came she was there to let them in.

"What's all the excitement?" Dugan ask.

She handed him the journal.

"You have found Raleigh's journal!"

"Yes and it is not damaged just faded a little. It can still be read." She said with enthusiasm.

"Where? Did you find anything else."

"Yes I have found it all, the paintings and the other treasures. I found them quiet by accident. I fell up the steps and one come lose and I could see light under a wall form the drama classroom. It is all there. Stored under the steps."

"May I see them?"

"Yes but we will have to have more light. My flashlight isn't enough."

Dugan went to his studio to get a light. When they turned on the light they couldn't believe all that was there.

"Look at that antique table. I will have it cleaned and put in the dance studio. It will be just right for the music. And if those chairs are not damaged we can use them in the classrooms."

"We will have to be careful when we start to take them down. They are stacked so high."

"I will help." Said Walter. "I can be careful. Lark always said there were treasures here."

"We will all help Walter." She said. "We will have to find a place to put them until we can get them cleaned.

"What about the bailey castle?" Dugan could hardly contain himself.

"I can take the paintings to my studio and clean them and look for Raleigh's signature on each one. You can come over and watch me and read the journal to me as I search for the signatures.

"What about comparing them to your paintings?"

"You can come over and help me look for the signatures and I would value your conception of the comparison. I have cleaned many old paintings."

"We will have to wait until the weekend when there are no students. I can hardly wait until we can get started."

Chapter Eighteen

The weekend had come and all the treasures were carried over to the bailey castle except the paintings. They were taken to the top of the tower and were in Dugan's studio.

Calista and Dugan were surprised at how gentle Walter was as he handled the treasures, as if he knew the value of each piece and what they would do to complete the restoration.

Ceara and Calista were working on the table for the music classroom. It was coming back to life and was a shinning beauty. No scratches and no damage had been done. The storage room had been dry or there would have been damage.

"We will take the vases to the kitchen and clean them next."

Walter came over and ask Calista. "If you will get me a tub of water and some cloths I will clean the chairs."

"That is a good idea Walter." She left the table and went to get what Walter wanted. She watched him and he was being careful and doing a good job.

"Where is Dugan?" Calista ask.

"He is over in his studio working on cleaning the paintings. He can't leave them alone. He was up most of the night looking at them and working. He Will soon have them ready to hang in the castle. He is in his glory with those paintings."

"I'm so anxious to see them and help him find Raleigh's signature on them." Calista said in a concerned voice. "He so much wants to compare them with his paintings and see how much of Raleigh's talent he inherited."

"Don't be surprised if his work is almost the same."

"Do you have enough students along that you can have a recital?"

"Oh yes, I have been giving them assignments to practice. I would like to have a recital soon. Some of them are getting really good. Their parents will be overjoyed with their progress. Those chairs will be a big help to seat their parents."

They finished up and walked over to the tower. Dugan was standing admiring the paintings. Ceara found her a chair and sit down to rest. Calista started to walk over to a painting Dugan had on an easel and cover with a cloth.

"No looking," he chided Calista. An artist covers his work when he don't want it to be seen until he is finished or plans an unveiling."

He handed the journal over to Calista.

"Read the names of the paintings to me as I try to fine the painting that goes with the name."

She read the name of the painting and Dugan attached a post-it to the frame.

"Do you want to search for the signatures at this time?"

"No let's wait until we have them all identified."

They had finished the clasification and had the painting of Buryl and Iola left. The painting was not listed in Raleigh's journal.

"Why would Raleigh not list this painting?" Calista asked in a confused voice.

"I don't know. Maybe he didn't paint it. If he had he would have listed it."

Ceara jumped up and went to look at the painting.

"He didn't paint it!" She said with enthusiasm. "One of his students must have painted it and gave it to him as a gift."

"You are right look at the brush stokes, they are not Raleigh's. Maybe the student gave it to Buryl and Iola as a gift knowing how Raleigh and Silvia felt. It may have hung in Buryl and Iola's living quarters. We will never know who painted it. But it is a very good likeness of them. Let's look for the signatures."

The three of them gathered around the paintings and with the journal they found the signatures. They were truly Raleigh's art work.

"Look." Calista said with excitement. "He has even made notation of where the paintings hung in the castle. He must have known someone would get the property and do the restoration."

"Good." Said Dugan. "That will make it much easier to hang them. Let's take the one of Raleigh and Silvia over and hang it above the fireplace."

The next day Calista went down and the portrait had been moved to another wall. She put it back over the fireplace and the next day it had been moved again. Who was moving the painting? She was determined to find out who was taking it down so she kept a close watch. Each day she watched and couldn't catch the culprit.

One morning she heard someone downstairs. And she startled Walter and he almost dropped the portrait.

"Walter what are you doing?" She had shouted and hadn't meant to. She was conscience-stricken when she saw the look on Walters face. She apologized immediately.

"Don't belong." He said in a sorrowful voice.

"But we have Raleigh's journal and it has the portrait hanging above the fireplace."

"No more." He hung it back on the opposite wall. "Don't belong. Not Raleigh's castle anymore. Your castle. You belong."

"You belong." He said over his shoulder as he walked out.

Calista didn't put the painting back over the fireplace. What was Walter thinking? Maybe Walter was right she did belong. This was now her place. I will have one of the best art students paint a portrait of me. I belong!

Chapter Nineteen

Calista was standing by the fireplace waiting on Walter and Dugan to come over. It was Christmas Eve and they were going to spend it together. Ceara had gone on a traveling trip with some of her friends and it would be just the three of them.

She had fixed a few snacks and some punch. It would be an enjoyable sharing the evening with them. Dugan had said he would have some stories to tell and some of them would be a surprise for her. He hadn't told any stories for awhile and she was anxious to hear them. Maybe it was stories from some of the Balthasar Christmases he had heard about also some from his family. She would like to hear some of Walters stories. Would he have some good memories of Christmases he spent with his mother before she became sick. Where he had spent the season and who with.

She wondered if the Hart family that the librarian was talking about ever spent time with him? In her heart she didn't think they had. If they had why would Lark and Aaron have looked after him after his mothers death? Had he spent his Christmases with a Lark and Aaron? Or had he spent them in the cave with no food or gifts.

She could tell some of her families Christmas stories also. How the families would sometimes spend a week together at her grandparents on the farm. The gathering would be filled with love, laughter, gift giving and food. They would take turns feeding the animals and helping their grandfather with the chores.

She heard someone at the door and went and peeped out.

"Walter is that you?" He wouldn't get to scold her this time.

"Yes it's me. I'm going over to the tower. Dugan wants me to help him with something. I'll be right back."

"Dugan is coming over why don't you come in where it's warm and wait for him?"

"I promised I would help him. I don't let promises go. I will come back with him when he comes."

"Alright but don't be long."

"We won't it's just a little job."

"Come on in when you come back. I'll be finishing up the snacks."

She went to the table and was fixing the punch when she heard them come in. Walter was giggling like a teenage girl and Dugan was shushing him. She heard Dugan whisper for him to be real still.

What were they doing? Calista heard a shuffling and movement. She couldn't stand it any longer she had to see what they were doing.

Dugan was hanging a large picture over the fireplace. Walter started clapping his hands.

"See I told you I could keep a secret. Come see, Calista, come see."

Dugan turned to look at her. Would she make him take it down? Or would she be surprised? Maybe he should have ask.

"I have painted you a portrait for Christmas. I hope you will like it."

"She will . . . she will." Walter was so excited.

She walked over and looked up at the image. It was beautiful and it was of her. She was standing on the knoll. She had on a soft gauzy dress and it was blowing in the wind. But the image standing beside her was a very soft shadow of a man with his hand resting on her shoulder. It was so faint she wondered if it was one of the Balthasar ghosts.

"What is the shadow? Is it one of the ghosts?"

"No it is your knight for the castle."

"I don't have a knight for my castle and may never have one."

"You will find one." Walter said with a warm glow around him. The fire was reflecting on him. He looked at Dugan. Dugan turned form the painting and looked at her.

"Walter and I have talked about this and we think you will find your knight. And just like the restoration it will be sooner than you think."

"But there is no one. Not at all like the restoration, with the restoration I had the ruins. Looking for a knight when there is no one." Calista laughed.

"When you find him and you will find him. I will take the painting and paint over the shadow and he will always be beside you."

"The portrait is lovely and so me. I like it very much. Let's go to the table."

"No" . . . Walter cried. "I have something for you."

He ran to the hall and came back with a gift rumpled and untidy. So what? It was the gift and not the paper right. She took the gift and ask.

"What is it Walter?"

"Open it . . . open it."

She opened the gift and couldn't believe the grace and delicacy of the gift. "Walter it is one of your rocks. It is so lovely."

"Your birthstone. I have been saving it for you."

She looked at Dugan with a questioning look. He shrugged his shoulder.

"I had nothing to do with this only bought the wood, stain and glue. Walter did it all by himself."

It was perfect. "Walter what a nice paper weight it will make for my desk. When I leave the window open sometimes my papers fly to the floor. This will hold them down. Every time I look at it I will think of you and how you love your rocks."

He beamed like a ray of sunlight.

"Now let's go to the table."

What a pleasure to watch Walter. He was like a little child as he enjoyed the food with a delightful happiness. Dugan whispered in her ear. "Bring your gifts that you have for him. We will go over to the bailey castle. I have more surprises for him."

Calista went to the sideboard and handed Dugan a gift. She had wrapped Raleigh's journal for Dugan. He is the one that should have it.

He was so surprised. He looked at her in amazement. "Christmas Eve what a night for surprises. I thought I would never see the journal again."

"It was your great grandfather's and it should be yours."

They put on their coats and walked to the bailey castle. Walter shivered as the cold wind blew snowflakes in his face.

"It' cold but I like snow." Walter was trying to catch the snowflakes inn his bare hands. Calista was so glad of the gifts she had bought. What was Dugan's surprise?

Dugan opened the door and pushed his way in first. He wanted to watch Walter and Calista's faces when they seen what he had done.

"Look around." And he swung his arms wide.

Calista also watched Walter as he examined the room. He beamed with emotional excitement as he looked around the room but all he saw was the murals on the walls. Then he turned to Dugan.

"You have painted my sea. Look at the mist as it comes off the waters. It is so real. And the cliffs. Oh, Dugan how did you do it?"

The picture of Walter Dugan had painted hung above the fireplace.

"It was easy Walter. I wanted you to be able to see it without going out in the cold. My best students helped me. There is more, come with me to the bedroom."

Dugan had built a fire in the fireplace and filled a wood rack. He had also put up a Christmas tree and decorated it. While Walter was following Dugan to the next room she slipped her gifts under the tree where Dugan had put more gifts. She hurried to catch them.

"You have painted my rocks and look there is my cave. Oh . . . oh just look."

He was touching the murals softly. Then he saw his blanket form the cave.

"This is my blanket. The one Lark gave me. Who took it from my cave?"

"I did Walter that is your bed. You will not have to sleep in the cold cave again."

"Never?"

"Never Walter this is where you are going to live from now on. Calista and I have talked about it and this is all yours."

"Walter is so happy." He said. "I want to look forever. It is so real. Will I never have to give it up?"

Calista came over to Walter and put her arms around him. "No Walter you will never have to give it up, you will never have to sleep in Aarons shed or the cave again. This is your home now. Let's go back in by the fire."

As they went back to the fire Walter saw the tree and ran to look at it.

"Is this Walters too?"

"Yes this is your too." Dugan smiled and patted his back.

"Is the gifts mine too?"

Calista shouted happily. "Yes let's open them."

"I haven't had gifts since my mom died. She used to get me pretty things and wrap then in pretty paper with bows."

Dugan waited till Walter sit down in the floor and he started to hand him one at a time the gifts he had brought.

He started to open them one at a time.

"New boots! New shirts! New pants! New socks! Walter will be warm now."

Calista got up and took the packages one at a time and handed them to him before he could get up off the floor.

"A new hat!" He put it on. "It even covers my ears."

He opened the next one Calista handed him without taking off the hat.

"New gloves! I have never had gloves before. Walters hands get so cold. Look Dugan new gloves."

Dugan nodded his head. He was enjoying this as much as Walter was.

Walter put the gloves on. Calista handed him a bigger package. He tried to open it without taking the gloves off but he couldn't. He didn't want to take them off but he wanted the package.

"A new coat! Now I can burn the old one."

He started to the fireplace but Dugan caught him before he left the floor.

"No Walter you can wear it when it isn't so cold. You can use it for a work coat."

Walter laid it down and smiled and put the new coat on. Walter jumped up and started dancing around the room. Going back and touching all his gifts again and again.

"Walter is so happy. Best Christmas ever."

Dugan pulled Calista to his side. She leaned her head on his shoulder. I have found my knight. She waited for her mothers words, but the room was so charged with excitement the words couldn't get through.

"Walter there is one more surprise I have for you."

Walter looked around and pointed to the tree. "No more packages."

"No this surprise isn't in a package."

Dugan pulled an envelop from his pocket, opened it and took out a paper and handed it to Walter.

"I can't read," he said and handed it to Calista. "You read."

"Walter this is your Birth Certificate."

"Birth Certificate? What is that?"

"Come over here I will show you. See right here it said Birth Certificate." She pointed to the words. "And here is you name."

Again she pointed to the words. Walter . . . Hart . . . Balthasar."

"Belthasar? I'm not a Balthasar."

Dugan stepped in. "Yes Walter you are a Balthasar. Your father and my father was the same man. I'm your half brother."

"Brother?"

"Half brother and Ceara is your half sister. She doesn't know this yet we will tell her when she comes back."

"Sister? I have a brother and a sister? Calista I have a brother and a sister!" A sorrowful, downcast look came to his face.

"What's the matter Walter? Does it not make you happy to have a half brother and sister."

"Calista I'm sorry. I have a brother and a sister and you don't have any."

"That's alright Walter. I have you, Dugan and Ceara and that is enough to make me happy."

The smile of excitement came back to his face.

"Best Christmas ever."

Printed in the United States
By Bookmasters